Lifeguards and Liars
A Nanny Blu Cozy Mystery

Summer in Diamond Bay
Book 1

By

Maci Grant

TABLE OF CONTENTS

CHAPTER 1

The rumble of the waves that crashed into the sand was punctuated by the laughter of children. Blu Parker took a deep breath of the salty air. She loved getting away from the busy city life to spend the summer at the beach house in Diamond Bay. It was one of the best perks of her current nanny job.

She watched Marley's damp blonde curls bounce as she ran back and forth across the sand in front of her. Joey threatened her with a fist full of wet sand.

"Joey! No throwing sand!" Blu's sharp voice shattered the otherwise peaceful beach.

Joey stuck out his tongue and puffed out his chest.

"Joey, put it down right this second!" Blu unwound herself from the comfortable position she'd settled into moments before and sprang to her feet.

Joey seemed to sense how thin her patience was as he dropped the mud. "She keeps trying to step on my castle! Make her stop!"

"I am not!" Marley stuck her hands on her hips.

"Here." Blu used her big toe to draw a wide circle around Joey's castle. "Marley, you're not allowed to go inside of this circle. Understand?" She met the four-year-old's bright blue eyes with her own.

"Okay." Marley stuck the tips of her toes at the edge of the line.

"Stop it!" Joey stomped his foot.

"I'm not in the circle!" Marley stuck out her tongue.

Blu took another deep breath of the salty air. "Look at that, Marley—a little crab." She pointed to the small creature that scuttled across the sand.

Marley chased after it, forgetting all about her brother's castle.

Joey was seven, lanky, and on the verge of being a teenager—according to him. He didn't have much patience for his little sister's antics. Blu looked forward to the two spending a little time apart when Joey would be going back to school at the end of summer. But summer had just begun, and Blu had to find creative ways to keep the siblings from torturing one another.

She settled back down on the beach blanket and glanced over at the lifeguard tower. She always tried to arrive early at the beach to get a spot near the lifeguard. She chose to be close, because she felt it was safer for the kids. Other nannies fought to be near the tower because of the bronzed god that perched atop it.

The pristine sand was dotted with other young

nannies all in perfect shape and unafraid to wear string bikinis, no matter how ridiculous they looked when they bounded after the toddlers they looked after. Blu, on the other hand, had never been able to wear anything other than a one-piece—she felt naked otherwise.

She dug her toenails into the sand to hide the paint job that Marley had done on her nails that morning. There was more polish on her toes than on her nails.

Marley ran by and whacked Blu's brown ponytail. Blu laughed and caught the little girl around the waist. She pulled her close and tickled her belly. As Marley squealed and broke free Blu was reminded of what a good life she lived. Most of the time she was surrounded by luxury and she got to spend her summers at the beach.

"Blu, want to go for a swim?" Joey looked up at her with one of his rare bright smiles.

"Sure, Joey. Let me wrangle Marley." She stood up and scooped up Marley before she could evade her. "Let's cool off in the waves for a bit."

"Careful now, there's a strong riptide."

His voice was as smooth as one of the waves that rolled in the distance. Blu squinted through the sunlight to smile at Sam, the lifeguard. "Thanks for the warning."

He nodded and returned his eyes to the water.

She could feel the jealous stares of the other girls. That's what they were to her—girls. At twenty-eight, Blu considered herself a nanny for life, while many of the others were just there for the summer—a way to help pay for college for many of them.

She shielded her green eyes and looked out at the other people in the water. It wasn't too crowded. She could see one familiar face. "Maddie! Hey, Maddie!"

Maddie ducked a big splash that a ten-year-old girl sent flying in her direction. Her black hair was soaked and her already tanned skin was baked even darker by the sunlight.

"She's trying to drown me, Blu!"

Sam stood up on the lifeguard stand. "Everything okay out there?"

For just a split second Maddie looked as if she might sink down into the water just to get his attention, but at the last moment she waved her hand to show that she was okay. Blu rolled her eyes. Maddie didn't care that she was twenty-seven and far too old to be lusting after a man barely out of his teens. Blu, Joey, and Marley waded their way into the water.

"Chrissa, stop it!" Maddie splashed the ten-year-old back.

"My hair, Maddie! What are you thinking!" Chrissa touched her glossy brown hair. "Really, you know better."

Blu cringed at the way Chrissa talked to Maddie. It wasn't unusual for spoiled kids to boss their nannies around, but Chrissa could be especially difficult to deal with.

"Well, if you don't want to get your hair wet, then maybe you shouldn't be in the water." Blu spoke in a polite but pointed tone to Chrissa.

"That's not really any of your business, is it?" Chrissa fluffed her hair, then she dove right into the next wave with no concern for her hair.

"Wow, she's in rare form today." Maddie rolled her eyes.

"Don't let it get to you, Maddie. Remember she's going to push all your buttons. You have to be able to keep your cool."

"I know, I know. I don't know how you've done it for so long. I mean, I'm just getting my feet wet, so to speak, and what has it been? Almost ten years for you?"

"Eight. I started nannying while I was in college to help pay my tuition."

"Right. I remember." Maddie laughed. "While I was busy trying to get Glenn to marry me, you were busy trying to become a journalist."

"You see how well that worked out for both of us." Blu grinned.

"Watch it! The divorce is still fresh!" Maddie laughed. "You're right, though. Who knew when we graduated high school that our lives would end up like this? I always thought we'd be the rich and the elite, not the ones raising their kids."

CHAPTER 2

Blu looked over at Marley and Joey wistfully. "They have their whole lives ahead of them. I always wonder where they'll end up."

"Hey, our lives aren't over! In fact, I have a date tonight with an investment banker."

"Liar!"

"What?"

"They're never investment bankers. Any guy that claims to be an investment banker is probably a teller or one of those fly-by-night stockbrokers."

"Oh, kill my dream, why don't you!" Maddie stuck out her tongue. "Doesn't matter—he's hot enough he could be a bus boy and I wouldn't care."

Blu rolled her eyes and splashed her friend. "I thought you were waiting for Sam?"

"Yes, well, Sam might be a bit young for me."

"Now you see it?"

"I'm not even sure if he's old enough to drink yet."

As if summoned by their conversation, Sam leaped down from the lifeguard tower and charged into the water. Blu turned to look in the direction he was headed. She saw that a young boy—about Joey's age—had been pulled past the waves.

"Maddie, watch Marley and Joey for me!"

"Sure. Why?"

Blu didn't take time to answer. She dove in and took off swimming toward the boy. She was much closer and could reach him much faster than Sam. As her arms swung through the water she could see that his head had started to bob. He was losing his ability to stay above the water.

She swam harder and faster. Then she felt the smooth skin of his arm. She grabbed it and pulled him close. The boy clung to her a little too tight. In his panic, he pulled at her neck and shoulders. She fought to keep them both above water. Just when she thought she would go under, a strong arm wrapped around her waist.

"It's alright, I'm here. You're safe."

Blu smiled with relief. Sam swam them back toward the shore with the boy tucked under his arm and Blu nestled against his side.

"I'm fine, I can swim from here." She started to pull away, but he held her tight.

"Not until we're on the sand."

Blu tried to ignore the impact of being held by Sam. No, she wasn't enamored with him, but she also wasn't immune to the way the warmth of his muscular chest made her forget about what had almost happened.

Once they were on the beach, Maddie and the kids rushed out of the water after them.

The boy's nanny ran toward him. "Joshua! I told you not to go out so far!"

"I'm sorry." He started to cry.

"Thank you so much." The young woman gushed at Sam. "You're a hero."

"I had some help." Sam winked at Blu. "But you should be more careful. He could have drowned you."

"I learned my lesson." Blu smiled in return.

"Are you okay?" Maddie gave her a quick hug.

"I'm fine."

As Sam walked away, Maddie leaned closer to her friend. "Oh, I bet you're more than fine. You got the royal treatment, hm?"

"Oh, Maddie!" Blu rolled her eyes.

"I'm bored. Can we go?" Chrissa flipped her hair over her shoulder, interrupting them.

"Sure, alright. Get your stuff." Maddie waved to Blu as she walked away.

Blu played in the sand with Joey and Marley as the afternoon hours faded away. She played beach volleyball with them toward the end of the day.

One of her goals as a nanny was always to keep the kids as active as possible. She'd been very active as a child and believed it was a great way to stay healthy and happy.

Joey sent the beach ball flying across the sand. Blu chased after it. It enlivened her to run, as she'd spent her entire high school years on the track team. She fetched the beach ball and turned back to the kids.

As she walked back across the sand, the sunset drew her attention. It was a beautiful evening for a walk on the beach.

Marley tugged at her hand. "I'm starving, Blu. Please, I'm so hungry!"

"We're going to go have dinner now. As soon as I find your brother's shoe." She shook out the beach blanket. In the sand she caught sight of the blue tip of a flip-flop. She reached down to dig it out of the sand. As she did, she heard a familiar voice.

She glanced up in time to see a woman beside the lifeguard tower. Her expensive dress had no place on the beach and she looked totally out of place. Though she wore a wide-brimmed black hat, Blu knew exactly who she was.

Penelope Ross—one of the wealthiest and high-powered female CEOs in America. But in that moment she seemed as enamored with Sam as Maddie was.

"Don't look, Blu, it's not your business." She tried to focus on folding up the blanket. The kids kicked small fountains of sand up into the air as they waited for her.

Blu's attention was split between them and Penelope. At first she assumed the banter between the man and woman was flirting, but as she gathered the last of the sand toys she heard their voices rise.

"Let's go, kids." She herded Marley and Joey toward

the car. As she walked, she could hear them arguing, but she couldn't hear what they were saying. She settled the kids in the backseat and stood up to look back at the beach.

Penelope stalked away from the lifeguard tower. Sam ran toward the water.

Whatever they'd been arguing about was over now.

CHAPTER 3

When they arrived back at the beach house, Blu was surprised to see Rachel Nickels' car parked in the driveway. She'd expected the kids' mom to be out at the fundraiser that was being held at the luxury beach club that night. Marley and Joey ran ahead of her and burst into the house through the side door that led into the kitchen.

"Watch the sand, watch the sand!" Rachel swept her dark red hair back into a quick knot at the back of her head.

Blu could tell from the tension in her employer's face that her day had been rough.

"I'm sorry, Rachel, I'll sweep it up as soon as I get them bathed."

"Don't bother, I'll do it." Her tone was short.

Blu frowned and hurried the kids up to their rooms. Once she had them bathed she walked back downstairs to prepare their meal.

Rachel was on the phone when Blu walked into the kitchen.

"Marshall, I don't know why you do this to me every summer. Every summer you insist that we come here to socialize with all your friends, and then every year you're too busy with work to join in."

Blu did her best to make herself invisible as she put water on the stove for spaghetti. Things had been tense between Rachel and Marshall for quite some time.

While the water heated, Blu grabbed a broom to sweep up the sand the kids had tracked in.

Rachel hung up the phone and picked up a spoon to stir the pot that didn't need to be stirred. "You know, you're so lucky, Blu."

She looked over at her boss. "Am I?"

"Sure. You've made it almost to thirty without having to deal with marriage nonsense."

Blu smiled and took the spoon out of Rachel's hand. "I know how rough summers can be. Why don't you and Marshall meet up in the city this weekend for some alone time?"

"But Saturday is your day off." Rachel frowned.

"I don't mind. Besides, there's a carnival in town that I was hoping to take the kids to. If that's alright with you?"

"It's more than alright." Rachel hugged her. "I don't know what I'd do without you, Blu."

The words hung in Blu's mind as Rachel walked off to call her husband back. Rachel always treated her like part of the family. She tossed the pasta into the pot and began to heat up some sauce to go with it.

"Blu, Blu, Blu!"

"Marley, Marley, Marley!"

"I can't find my tiger."

"Oh, no! There's a tiger on the loose? What if he eats us?"

"Silly!" Marley giggled. "It's just a stuffed tiger."

"Oh, good. Maybe we can find him after dinner?"

"Okay." Marley nodded.

Blu hummed under her breath as she finished preparing the meal.

That night as she settled into bed, Blu thought again about Penelope on the beach. She'd arranged for Maddie to work for the Rosses as Maddie's first real nanny job. Now she hoped that Maddie wasn't in for more drama than she could handle.

Blu closed her eyes and recalled the phone call she'd received from Maddie nearly a year ago.

"My life is over, Blu. It's over."

"No, it's not, Maddie. I promise, it's not."

"How could he do this to me? He left me and now I have nothing."

"Don't worry, we're going to get you back on track. You're better off without him. He's a liar, a cheater, and he never treated you right."

"I know all of those things, so why doesn't it hurt any less?"

"I don't know. I'm sorry." That was the truth. Blu didn't know. She'd never been married—or even in love. She didn't know what it was like to have her heart broken. She was grateful for that, although she did fall asleep with the memory of Sam holding her close playing through her mind that night.

She barely had her eyes open when her phone began to buzz. She grabbed it off the nightstand.

"Hello?"

CHAPTER 4

"Oh my God, Blu, did you hear?"

She vaguely registered Maddie's voice in her ear.

"Did I hear what? I'm not even awake yet, Maddie. What are you talking about?"

"They just found Sam on the beach."

"Okay—they found a lifeguard on the beach..."

"Yes, but he's dead! Blu, Sam's dead."

"Wait, what?" She sat upright in her bed and rubbed at her eyes. "I'm sorry I, thought you said that Sam is dead."

"He is, Blu. They found him this morning. I can't even think about it without tearing up."

"How?" She blinked a few times to wake herself up. "How did he die?"

"He drowned. He still had his surfboard attached to his ankle. The rumor is that he went out for an early morning ride on the waves and just didn't come back."

"Wow. That's terrible."

"It is terrible. I think I'm going to keep Chrissa and Brennan away from the beach for a while."

"That's probably a good idea. How is Penelope?"

"She was gone early this morning. Why do you ask?"

"Oh, I just saw her on the beach last night talking with Sam. I thought maybe she'd be upset."

"Penelope? You must have been mistaken. She was out of town yesterday for a business meeting. Even if she had been in town, she wouldn't have been on the beach talking to Sam—or any lifeguard, for that matter."

"Maybe I'm mistaken." Blu frowned. She didn't think that she was mistaken at all, but there wasn't much point in arguing with Maddie over it.

"Chelsea is planning a beach memorial already. You know how she likes to throw parties."

Blu rolled her eyes at the thought of the young nanny, Chelsea, turning a tragic death into a party opportunity. Chelsea threw a party every chance she got. They were always elaborate and over the top.

"I still don't understand how Sam could have died. He's an amazing swimmer. You saw the rescue yesterday. How does someone like that die in the water?"

"I don't know. Maybe he passed out, or maybe he slipped? Maybe he just had a little too much to drink."

"That early in the morning, though?"

"All I know for sure is that he died, and the locals around here are devastated. You know how well liked he was."

"Yes I do." Blu frowned. She glanced at the time and then sighed. "I have to get the kids up and going. They have swim lessons at the beach today."

"Ugh. Good luck. Bettina is vicious."

"I know it, but she's the best."

"So they say." Maddie hung up.

Blu hustled out of bed and got dressed. She woke the children with the same lighthearted song that she always sang in the morning. They were grumpy, but managed to rummage around to find their swimsuits. While they dressed, Blu prepared a quick breakfast of sliced fruit and yogurt.

"Morning, Blu." Rachel drifted into the kitchen.

Blu pushed the button on the coffee maker. "Morning. How are you, Rachel?"

"Okay." She smiled. "Are you sure about this weekend?"

"Absolutely."

"I really appreciate it." She flipped on the television.

"Oh, uh, better not." Blu picked up the remote and turned the television off.

"Why? You know I like to catch the morning news."

"It's best that the kids don't see it this morning." Blu leaned in closer and spoke to Rachel in a low voice. "There was an accident on the beach."

"Accident?"

Before Blu could answer, Rachel's phone buzzed with a text message. She looked at the screen and then gasped.

Blu nodded. "It might be best if we try to keep the kids from finding out."

"You're absolutely right." She shook her head and started typing away on her phone.

Blu hurried the kids through breakfast. They kissed their mother goodbye and headed out for their swim lessons.

The drive to the beach was only two minutes long. If the kids had more endurance, Blu would have them walk. But as it was, she knew that Joey would be tired after class and Marley was getting a little too big to carry.

She parked in the small lot near the dock where the swim lessons were to take place.

As soon as they were out of the car, the kids raced toward the water, calling out to their instructor, "Morning, Bettina!"

Bettina stood at the edge of the water. She wore a bright blue whistle around her neck and had an orange kickboard tucked under her arm. "Move it, move it, move it!" she called out to the kids.

Blu did her best not to roll her eyes. Even when they were right on time, Bettina was difficult to deal with, but when they were a few minutes late, she was impossible.

As Blu scanned the kids in the water she noticed that there weren't as many as usual. "Morning, Bettina. I guess that we're not the only ones who are late this morning." Blu set down her folding chair in the sand not far from the edge of the water.

"No, you're the only one that's late. The others aren't coming." Bettina pointed to the two kickboards that were waiting for Joey and Marley.

"What? So many? Why not?" Blu settled into her chair.

"Because of the news about Sam—I assume you heard?"

Blu nodded as Bettina continued.

"Now everyone's concerned about the safety of the children. Some of them are worried that the riptide is too strong. Others are just creeped out by the idea of the kids being in the water near where Sam died."

"Huh." Blu narrowed her eyes. "That doesn't make much sense to me. If the riptide is bad, then the kids need to know how to deal with it. And if someone like Sam could die in that water, then yes—they need all the skills they can get."

"Exactly my point, but you know how these families can be." Bettina lowered her voice. "Sometimes a good dose of reality sends them running."

CHAPTER 5

Blu nodded without responding verbally to Bettina. She did her best not to speak poorly about her employers or about anyone in their circles, really. Being a nanny was more than just a job. She knew that it took a lot of trust for someone to invite a stranger into their home and expect them to help raise their children. It was joining a family, if only for a short time, and she would not violate that trust—not for anything.

"What do you mean by a dose of reality?"

"Well, it's obvious that Sam must have been high or drunk. I mean, I checked the reports this morning around four—I do that every morning before class. The water was calm, no reports of bad weather, no rogue waves— even the riptide isn't so bad today. Yet by six in the morning, Sam was dead. The only way that's possible is if he got plastered and then got on a surfboard, right? But now, to all of these people he was an angel, a saint, a protector of their children, and this event is equal to the assassination of a president." She rolled her eyes and glanced at the water. "The ocean doesn't care who you are. If you're not careful, you'll lose your life."

"Sam didn't seem the type to drink though, Bettina. I never noticed him being anything other than alert."

"Well, if that argument on the beach last night was any proof, I'd say he had a lot on his mind."

"You mean with Penelope?"

"Huh?"

Blu bit her tongue. She realized that she'd broken her own rule. "Who did you see him arguing with on the beach last night?"

"I take a last jog along the beach around eight. It was just dark, and I didn't even see them at first. I heard them."

"Who?"

"It was Sam and a man. The man sounded really angry. He must have been rich."

"Why do you think that?"

"Oh, he kept threatening to get him fired—to sue him, to ruin his life. You know—the usual wealthy intimidation. My guess is that Sam got stressed out, had too much to drink, and got himself killed." She frowned. "Sure it's sad, but it's real life."

"Do you know who the man was?"

"No, I didn't see his face. His voice sounded familiar, but to be honest, I rarely get to know anyone but nannies and the occasional mother."

"Do you know what the man was angry about?" Blu scooted forward to the edge of her chair, her curiosity more than a little piqued by this time.

"Who knows? Maybe he owed money, maybe his dog pooped on the wrong lawn, right?" She laughed. "Anyway, all that matters now is that he's dead. Whatever that man wanted from Sam, he's not going to get it now." Bettina stopped abruptly. "I have to get in the water." She turned and ran into the waves with the kids.

Blu sat back in her chair and stared out over the water. Normally, she'd watch the kids' lesson with interest, but her mind was on other things. Her thoughts kept turning back to Sam. He was so watchful, so dedicated to his job, and so cautious about the water. She found it very difficult to imagine him being so reckless.

She closed her eyes for a moment and recalled the argument that she'd witnessed. She was sure that it had been Penelope Ross that she saw on the beach with Sam. But Maddie had insisted that Penelope was out of town.

It had been dusk and Blu had been distracted by the kids. Maybe she was wrong.

What she knew for sure was that Sam had been in an argument with a woman, then only an hour or so later, he'd also had an argument with a man. Sam had some people upset with him. Was that really enough to drive him into making such a stupid decision?

"Look at me, Blu! Look at me!" Marley kicked her feet as fast as she could.

"Good job, Marley!" Blu waved to her and smiled. She lost herself in pride for a moment as she watched

Joey's strong strokes. The summer before, he could barely doggie paddle and Marley wouldn't even go near the water. It was amazing to her how fast children grew and changed.

As the lesson ended, Bettina struck up a conversation with another of the nannies, who had arrived to pick up her charges. Blu overheard them talking about Sam.

She rushed the kids to the car to keep them from hearing too much. Innocence only lasted so long, and she wanted to keep theirs intact for as long as she could.

As she drove them back to the beach house she noticed a flower delivery van pass her, headed toward the beach. She guessed it was going there to set up for Chelsea's memorial.

As if on cue, her phone buzzed.

She parked in the driveway before checking the message. It was from Chelsea.

Memorial today to honor our fallen hero.

It listed the time, appropriate attire, and a note saying that donations would be accepted for the family.

Normally, Blu might have been disgusted by Chelsea's using a death as an excuse to throw a party, but she decided she wanted to go for two reasons. First, she wanted to show support for Sam's family and friends. Secondly, she wanted to see if the woman or man he'd argued with the night before would show up.

She got the kids bathed and started preparing their lunch.

While they watched a cartoon, Blu texted Maddie to see if she'd be going to the memorial.

I'm not sure. Penelope came home early and she's in a mood. I'll let you know.

Blu stared at the message. Was Penelope home early because she'd never actually left?

CHAPTER 6

Blu decided to see if she could find out a little more information about Sam. In her classes at college she'd learned quite a bit about how to search for information.

As she poked around through Sam's life online, her throat grew dry. Was it wrong to be so invasive? He had saved her life just the day before. Now she was trying to dig up dirt on him?

It was not hard for her to crack the password on his local bank account—younger people really weren't that inventive when it came to such things. She saw that he had very little money. Was that because he had a low salary or had he just taken out a large amount? His bank account didn't show her much other than his paychecks and frequent purchases at the local diner.

His social media accounts were rather sparse for a guy his age—not many selfies posted at all—something that Blu could actually appreciate. He did have some accounts, but they were neglected and out of date.

About the only thing she could find about him was an article written in the local newspaper about his dedication to the safety of the beachgoers. It somehow made her more sad that he'd barely left his mark on the world. He was too young to be gone.

Rachel arrived home just after Blu had fed the kids lunch and gotten Marley settled for a nap.

"I'd like to spend some time with the kids this afternoon. Will that interrupt your day?"

"Not at all. We didn't have anything planned."

"Great, then you can have the afternoon and evening off. I know you'll probably want to go to the memorial. I'd appreciate it if you took a check for me to put in for the donation. I just can't tolerate gloomy things. Does that make me terrible?"

Blu smiled at her employer's insecurity. Rachel had no reason to be insecure. She was intelligent, attractive, and wealthy. Yet, she seemed to always be looking to Blu for reassurance. Blu didn't mind. She knew what it was like to be uncomfortable in her own skin.

"No, it doesn't make you terrible. I think it's better that the kids are with you on a day like this. I'm sure that his family will appreciate your donation."

"Any little bit helps, right?" She pulled her checkbook out of her purse. She wrote out one amount and then Blu noticed her add another zero to the end. The sharp tear of the check startled Blu out of her thoughts. "Here you go."

"Thanks, Rachel. That's very generous of you."

"No amount of money brings back a life, though,

does it?" She frowned. "I saw him just the other day too. He was in the post office with his girlfriend."

"Girlfriend? I didn't know that Sam had a girlfriend."

"Well, I assumed that she was. They were holding hands. Then again, I guess at his age he might have had a few girlfriends."

"Do you remember what she looked like?"

"Yeah, she was tiny and blonde—you know, the kind of girl that belongs at the top of a cheerleading pyramid. I thought they made a cute couple."

Blu nodded. "I'm sure they did."

Before heading to the memorial, Blu walked into the center of the small beach town. On one side of the town were all of the stores and shops that catered to the wealthy. On the other side of town were the shops and stores that were owned and used by the locals.

Blu headed for the local side.

There wasn't a visible division between the two, but where the sidewalk ended was usually where the wealthy didn't venture. She didn't really visit this area either, as it wasn't where most of the shops and places she took the kids were.

A few people stood outside a convenience store as she approached. One was an older man, the other was a lanky teenage boy.

"Good afternoon." She nodded to them.

"What's so good about it?" The teenage boy wiped at

his eyes.

"Sorry, miss, he's just upset." The older man put his hand on the boy's shoulder. "He was one of Sam's junior lifeguards."

"I'm very sorry. It was a tragic accident." Blu frowned.

"They're all lying!" The boy stood up from the wall of the building and glared at her. "It wasn't an accident! Sam would never have gone in the water if it weren't safe. I know that someone did this to him!"

"Tommy, you've got to calm down. This lady has nothing to do with any of this. Please excuse him, miss, he watches too many of those detective television shows."

"She is exactly who is involved with this. Who else do you think would murder someone and make it look like an accident? You work for one of the rich summer families, don't you? Which one of them murdered my friend?"

Blu took a slight step back. "I'm sorry, I don't know what you're talking about."

"Tommy, that's enough!" The older man scowled at him. "Those tourists keep this town afloat. Have some respect. You're going to have to let go of this nonsense. Chief Pitman already told you that there was no sign of foul play. What more has to be done to prove you wrong?"

"Wait." Blu reached out and touched Tommy's arm. "I found it hard to believe too, Tommy. He was such a skilled swimmer—and a good person. I can see why you're upset and why you want to believe that it isn't true."

"It's not true!" Tommy shook her hand away. "It's an outright lie. Now the town will go on believing that Sam was reckless or stupid. He was my teacher. He taught me about the power of the water—and to always respect it. He made sure that we all understood that the moment we stepped in the water, we put our lives at risk." He took a deep breath and shook his head. "He was always smart enough not to make any bad decisions. But this—this isn't how he was supposed to die. It just isn't fair."

The older man grabbed him by the curve of his neck and pulled his head against his shoulder.

"I know it, Tommy, I know it. But harassing this woman isn't going to change anything. Inventing a murder isn't going to bring Sam back."

CHAPTER 7

The word "murder" hung in the air as Blu stepped past the two and into the store. There were a few more people inside, though none appeared to be shopping. It looked more like they were just sharing conversation. Blu noticed the girl behind the counter appeared to be about Sam's age. She had red hair and her eyes were swollen— as if from crying, Blu guessed.

"Hello." Blu set down a pack of gum on the counter.

"Hi," the girl squeaked out. She rang up the gum. "Seventy-nine cents."

Blu pulled out a dollar and handed it to her. "Are you going to the memorial tonight?"

"I doubt it. We're not usually invited to that sort of thing."

"What do you mean?"

"Have you seen what they've done to the beach?" She shook her head. "Sam would be livid over all of those decorations cluttering the sand. He hated parties on the beach, even when it was just us locals with a fire pit."

"I didn't know that about him. Did his girlfriend feel

the same way?"

"Girlfriend?" The girl brushed her hair back over her shoulders. "Oh, you mean Kayla?" She shook her head. "No, they would argue about it sometimes. Kayla liked to party and have fun, Sam was just always thinking ahead. I guess that's why they broke up."

"They broke up recently?" Blu took her change from the girl.

"Yeah—just a few days ago. Kayla was real upset. She and Sam had been together since grade school."

"Did they fight a lot?"

"Never. In fact the break-up surprised her so much that she thought he was joking. She got really upset when he made it clear that he wasn't."

"Hm. Why do you think they broke up?"

"Why do you want to know?" She stared hard at Blu. "Are you writing an article or something? Maybe you should write about all the things the women on the other side of town tried to get him to do. That's probably why they broke up."

"Oh, was Sam seeing someone else?"

"Look. I'm not going to say anything bad about a dead man. Sam was a good guy. But he fell on some hard times. I know he needed money and I know he had a lot of offers on the table. That's all I'm going to say."

"Offers?" Blu shook her head, hoping she could get just a little more information out of the girl. "What do you mean?"

"For private parties—you know—personal attention. They hide it well, but those women are wild. You should know." She smirked. "Or maybe that's why you're asking?"

"No, not at all." Blu frowned and picked up her pack of gum. "Thanks. If you don't mind, where do you think I can find Kayla? I'd like to give her my condolences."

The girl looked at her for a moment and then nodded. "She'll be at the Beach Bum."

"Thanks." Blu turned and walked out of the convenience store.

Tommy and his father were gone. In fact, the entire street was empty. Could Sam's death really have been a murder? She hated to think about the possibility, but there it was right in front of her. Tommy made a lot of sense, and it seemed that everyone who knew Sam didn't believe it was an accident.

She walked down the road toward the bar. Several of the nannies enjoyed their weekends off there. She knew it had a reputation for being a little rowdy, but nothing too out of hand. She had never been to it, but here was a first for everything.

When she reached the Beach Bum, she took a look at its plain exterior. It was blue—perhaps in an attempt to match the water—with no windows on the front. The only thing that indicated its name was a small placard above a plain wooden door.

Blu pulled open the door to the bar. It was still pretty

early in the afternoon, so she didn't expect to see many people inside. The light was dim, some classic rock played on the radio, and there was a distinct smell of peanuts and beer. Blu hadn't been in a bar since her college years, and even then, she hadn't spent much time in them. She blinked a few times to adjust to the light.

"Can I help you?"

Somehow she hadn't noticed the man until he was standing right in front of her. The first thing she saw was the large metal keg in his hands. Then her gaze followed his hands up along his thick muscular arms.

When her eyes made their way to his face, she had to take a slight step back. He was handsome in a rugged way, with a crooked nose, rough square lips, and a few wayward locks of dark brown hair splayed across his forehead. But there was something about him, something past his face, past his half-smile, past even the glimmer in his dark eyes, that gave her a jolt.

Was it familiarity? Had she seen him somewhere before? At the grocery store? On the beach?

"We're not actually open for business at the moment." He squinted at her. "Did you want a drink or something?"

Blu realized she'd been staring at him for much longer than was appropriate.

"Oh, I'm sorry. The door was open, so I just assumed…" She shook her head. "I don't need anything." She started to turn away, but noticed a petite blonde sitting at the end of the bar. She paused. "Actually, maybe I could have a beer?" She thought asking for a water would be strange.

"Sure, no problem. Just give me a minute."

CHAPTER 8

The guy lugged the keg behind the bar.

Blu tried not to notice the way his muscles rippled beneath his tight t-shirt. It was odd to her to notice a man this way, as most of the time one man was just like another to her—something to admire from a distance. She continued to watch him as she took a seat beside the other woman at the bar. The guy could have been in his late twenties, but it was possible that he was older—not that it mattered.

"Bottle or glass?" He looked across the bar at her.

"Bottle."

"Light or dark?"

Blu scrunched up her nose. "Dark, I guess."

He tilted his head to the side and fixed her with a look. Then he put a bottle of beer down in front of her. "You look like a red."

"A red?" She glanced over at the blonde beside her. She had a frothy beer in front of her. Blu fought the urge to ask her if she was old enough to drink.

"Beer." He grinned. "It's a type of beer."

"Oh, okay." Blu managed a smile. When it came to social interaction, especially when she didn't expect it, she often struggled with the right thing to say. "Thanks." She pulled out some money to pay for the beer.

"No, sorry, can't accept that since we're not actually open. Besides, on a day like today, we all need a drink."

Blu was surprised. She kept the money gripped tightly in her hand. Then she turned to look at the woman beside her.

"Kayla?"

The woman turned to look at her. "Excuse me?"

"I'm sorry. I thought you might be someone I was looking for."

"My name is Shawna. Kayla left a little while ago." She stood up from the bar. "I guess she's the town celebrity right now."

"Why do you say that?"

"Because Sam is dead. Now everybody feels bad for her."

"Shawna." The man behind the bar spoke with a warning tone in his voice.

"What?" Shawna shrugged. "I thought this was the one place in this ridiculous town that I could tell the truth without getting shushed by the powers that be."

"I'm not shushing you, I just think you should be careful."

"Of her?" Shawna grinned at Blu. "Oh, he must think you're one of the fancy ladies. I can see why—in that pants suit." She giggled.

Blu looked down at the hunter green outfit she wore. It was technically a hand-me-down from her employer. She thought it would be appropriate for the memorial.

"But you're not, are you?" Shawna leaned closer to her. "You're just the help."

"Shawna, cut it out." The man behind the bar leaned his hands on the top of it and glared at Shawna.

"It's true. You just gave a freebie to a nanny." She laughed.

"My name is Blu." She looked from Shawna to the bartender. "And she's right, I am a nanny. I'm sorry if I gave you the wrong impression. I'm happy to pay for the beer."

"Don't listen to her nonsense. I don't care who you are or what you do." He held out his hand to her. "I'm AJ."

Blu smiled and shook his hand. The moment she touched his hand she felt that familiar jolt again. She pulled her hand away and looked at her beer.

"Are you going to drink that?" He grinned.

She picked it up and took a sip. For beer, it was quite good.

"So why were you looking for Kayla?" Shawna turned on her stool to face Blu.

"I'm not sure really. I heard that she was Sam's girlfriend. I guess I wanted to tell her how sorry I am for her loss."

"Oh, did you know Sam?" Shawna crossed her legs. "Most of the nannies do."

"No. Not really. But he saved me yesterday, along with a young boy. It's so sad."

"It is." AJ nodded. "Sam will be missed."

"Especially by Kayla. Poor girl got sideswiped by him dumping her and now she'll never have the chance to set things right with him," Shawna said.

"Why did they break up?"

Shawna pursed her lips. She looked over at AJ for a moment and then back to Blu. "I'm not sure. He told her that he thought they just needed a break. Yeah, right." She rolled her eyes.

"Shawna."

"AJ, it's a bunch of BS. You and I both know that he was hooking up with someone else."

"I'm sorry, my little sister is not one to respect the privacy of others." AJ shook his head.

"Oh, it's fine. Who keeps secrets around here?" Blu smiled. "I did hear something rather troubling, though."

"What's that?" AJ rested his hands on the bar again.

"Well, there was this boy outside the convenience store. Tommy?"

"Oh, Tommy." Shawna cringed. "Yeah, he's taking it very hard—poor kid."

Blu didn't point out that he was only a few years younger than Shawna. "He seems to think that maybe it wasn't an accident."

"You be careful what you say." AJ's friendly demeanor vanished.

Blu looked at him with surprise, in that his attitude could change so fast and that he took the liberty of speaking to her so sharply.

"Excuse me?"

"You're a nanny. You should know better. Rumors like that can get you fired."

"What rumors?"

AJ's jaw seemed to clench tighter. He picked up a rag and began wiping down the already clean bar.

"Tommy's not the only one who thinks that something else happened to Sam." Shawna stood up from the bar stool as she spoke. "But what does it matter? No one is ever going to consider it anything more than an accident. Money covers up everything around here."

"Are you saying that you think someone wealthy did this?" Blu looked over at AJ, who turned his back to her.

"What do you think, AJ?" Shawna smiled. "What does good old Uncle Paul have to say about it?"

"Shawna. Seriously, drop it. If there was any evidence he'd be looking into it."

"Would he?" Shawna shook her head. "Forget the beer. I'm going to meet up with some friends." She turned and walked out of the bar.

CHAPTER 9

"Uncle Paul?" Blu took another sip of her beer as she directed the simple question to AJ.

"He's the police chief." AJ shrugged. "Shawna and several of her friends have a theory that Sam got involved with the wrong person and ended up dead. You know—they're young, they're looking for drama."

"And you, AJ? What do you think happened to Sam?"

AJ grimaced. "I think that it doesn't matter and looking into it can only make things worse."

"Really?" Blu frowned. "You don't care if he was murdered?"

"Of course I care. I just know that nothing will be done about it."

"Please, the wealthy go to jail too."

"Not in this town they don't." AJ picked up his sister's untouched beer and drank it down. "Trust me, Blu, it's better this way."

Blu stood up. "I don't think so. If there's a chance that Sam was murdered, then someone should be looking into it."

"No one will." He met her eyes.

"I will." Blu set the money she still clenched in her hand down on the bar. "I'm not going to let a man's death be swept under the rug because it's the convenient thing to do."

AJ looked from the money to her. "Good luck. Don't say I didn't warn you." He turned away and completely ignored the money on the bar.

Blu bit the tip of her tongue to keep from telling him what she thought of his opinion. One of the biggest issues she'd faced while studying journalism was the concept that the truth was sometimes better left undiscovered. Yet she couldn't help herself for needing to find out the truth.

Her heart pounded as she walked out of the bar. She could hear music drifting from the beach. Her stomach churned.

What if Shawna was right? Sure, some of the wealthy that she'd encountered acted as if they were above the law—but murder? Why would anyone want Sam dead?

When she arrived at the beach, she made her way to the section that had a black and red ribbon marking a good portion of it.

A security officer stopped her from entering into the area.

"Private memorial service."

Blu raised an eyebrow. "This is a public beach."

"Today it's private."

Chelsea bounded over with a wide smile on her face. "It's alright, James, she's on the list." Chelsea waved Blu past the ribbon.

Blu shook her head. "Chelsea, you've outdone yourself."

"Oh really, do you think?" She smiled proudly. "Whatever I can do to give back, you know?"

"Oh, that reminds me." Blu reached into her purse and pulled out the check. "Rachel wanted to contribute to the fund for the family. It is for the family, right?"

"Yes, of course, and boy, do they need it. Sam's parents couldn't even afford the flight to come to the memorial."

"He's not from here?"

"He is, but his parents moved a few states away. I guess they lost their house or something." She shrugged. "You know how that goes. Anyway, they'll be rolling in it now, won't they?" She winked.

Blu swallowed back her disgust. It was hard to stomach Chelsea's perky nature at a memorial. But she knew it wasn't intentional. That was just how Chelsea was—always perky.

"Did you invite some of the locals?"

"No, why would I do that?"

"Because he grew up here. He lived and worked here."

"Oh, I know, and I'm sure they'll do their own memorial at some point. I mean, why wouldn't they if they cared about him? But this is more for those lives he touched—you know, those of us from the summer homes."

"I see." She did her best not to say another word. There was no reason to argue the point.

As Blu walked further along the sand she saw several white chairs set up, as well as speakers that played sad soft music. There were flowers on the ribbon, and flowers that littered the sand. When she saw the balloons tied to some of the chairs she cringed. Balloons by the water? It seemed like a very bad idea.

"Hey, Blu!" Maddie walked over to her. "Can you believe this?"

"I don't think I want to."

"I know, it's over the top as usual. I've heard she's got some seagulls somewhere that she plans to release."

"How are you? Is everything okay with Penelope?"

"Penelope? Oh, yes. She's just in a mood. She didn't want to come to the memorial, so she's at home with the kids. Brian brought me." She smiled proudly.

"He brought you?"

"You know—he drove me. I guess he wanted to represent the family."

Blu looked past Maddie to Brian Ross. He was dressed in a dark suit with his hands clasped behind his back as he spoke quietly to another man. Blu shivered slightly.

For some reason Mr. Ross always intimidated her.

She'd covered for their old nanny a few times, and every time, she'd done her best to avoid Brian Ross. Maybe it was just his height and girth that made her uneasy. Or perhaps it was the way he looked at her while she played with the kids in the pool.

"How are the kids handling it? Did you tell them?"

"Penelope thought we should. Chrissa thought it was a big joke. She started talking about how the beach will be haunted now. Brennan locked himself in his room." She sighed. "He's getting worse, I think."

"Twelve is a tough age for any kid."

"I guess. Maybe if Brian spent more time with him…"

"Good luck. Brian seems to think his role is strictly management. I've never seen him play with the kids."

"You'd think with Penelope being the one that makes all the money, he'd be more available to the kids."

"Hello, ladies. Not talking about me, I hope?" Brian stepped up beside them.

Maddie's face drained of all color and Blu quickly spoke, hoping he wouldn't notice. "No, not at all, Mr. Ross."

"Blu, I do wish you'd call me Brian. We've been over this, haven't we?"

Blu nodded.

"She's very polite." Maddie offered Brian a sunny smile.

Blu noticed that Maddie touched the slope of Brian's

forearm.

"I'm going to take my seat. Want to join me?" Brian looked at Maddie. "Blu, you should sit with us a well."

"Thanks, I think I'll do that." Blu narrowed her eyes. "I just need to speak to Maddie for another moment, if you don't mind?"

"No problem." He walked over to the front row of chairs.

CHAPTER 10

"Maddie!"

"What?" Maddie smiled.

"Just what do you think you're doing with Brian?"

"Huh? Nothing. He's so nice, don't you think?"

"He's also married—and your boss."

"Blu, don't be such a prude. Nothing is happening between us."

"I warned you before I got you the job with them—it's easy to get too close and too personal. What do you think Penelope would say if she saw you touching his arm like that?"

"Oh, please—like she would even notice. She's barely home and when she is, she doesn't pay Brian any attention. The poor man is lonely, can't you see it?"

Blu looked over at Brian. He had his phone out. "Sure. They're all lonely when they're interested in the help."

"Oh, stop worrying, I'm not going to do anything stupid. I promise."

Blu met her friend's eyes. She wanted to believe her, but her gut told her differently. Maddie had been ruined by a man who took everything from her. Brian could give her everything she ever dreamed of having. And he wasn't exactly hard to look at.

"Just be careful, Maddie. I don't know Penelope very well, but I do know that she's a powerful woman. I don't want you to get into something you can't get out of."

"Trust me, Penelope has her own fun."

"What does that mean? You think she's cheating on Brian?"

Maddie shrugged. "I don't know for sure, but she's not buying fancy lingerie to wear for Brian."

"Maddie, that's being way too involved!"

"I can't help it, she has me go to the store and pick up the stuff she orders. I have to check to make sure it's right. Anyway, let's just drop it. Today isn't about the problems in their marriage, it's about Sam."

Blu glanced over at Brian again.

She was certain that she'd seen Penelope on the beach the night before with Sam. Was he the person that she'd been having an affair with? Shawna had mentioned that there were rumors about his being with someone else.

"Some of the locals think that maybe Sam's death wasn't an accident," Blu whispered to Maddie.

"Really?" Maddie's eyes widened. Then she shook her head. "That's just not possible. It's clear that he drowned. How else could he have died?"

"I don't know. Let's go, it's starting."

Blu made a point of sitting between Maddie and Brian. To anyone else it might have looked like she was trying to be close to Brian, but she was only trying to keep rumors from buzzing about her friend.

It was tough being a nanny sometimes, and keeping enough distance from the family was even harder. She had no problem keeping her distance from Brian—or Marshall for that matter, especially since Marshall was rarely home.

The memorial started out as expected—Chelsea, with tissue in hand, talking about what an amazing person Sam had been. Blu wasn't sure if Chelsea and Sam had ever even had a conversation, but the speech was touching nonetheless.

Just as Chelsea was finishing, there was a wild shriek from the back of the chairs. Blu turned around to see a very tiny blonde woman with her face twisted into an angry grimace.

"What do you know about him? What do you know?"

"That must be Kayla."

"Kayla?" Maddie leaned close.

"Sam's girlfriend."

"Oh." Maddie frowned. "She looks a little upset."

"This should be interesting." Brian turned around in his chair to watch.

Kayla stalked toward the podium.

"You! I don't even know who you are! How can you

know who Sam is? Why are you doing this without his family here? Who do you think you are?" She nearly screamed as she stalked right up to Chelsea.

Chelsea's perky smile faded. "We all loved Sam."

"Oh, you did?" Kayla spun around and stared at the people gathered before her. "You all loved Sam? No! I loved Sam! I did! I've loved him since we took our first surfing lesson together. None of you loved him. You took him from me!" Kayla started sobbing.

"It was an accident—a terrible, tragic accident!" Someone called out.

"Sure." Kayla rolled her eyes. "You know something? If Sam were here right now, he'd throw all of you off his beach!" She kicked some sand into the air and stalked off.

"Well, that was shocking." Maddie shook her head.

Chelsea wiped her eyes and began to speak about tragedy again.

"Excuse me." Blu stood up and slipped past Maddie.

"Where are you going?" Maddie looked up at her.

"I'm just going to take a walk."

Maddie shrugged and shifted into the seat that Blu had vacated. Blu cringed as she noticed the arm that Brian wrapped around her friend's shoulders.

She followed the footsteps that Kayla had left behind in the sand. She did her best to keep her distance so as not to spook the young woman. It was clear that she was upset about Sam's death, but Blu detected more anger than grief in her.

When she rounded the corner behind the small building that housed showers and bathrooms, she heard Kayla's voice.

"Can you believe those nuts? Whatever. Here. This is the other half of what I promised you. Make yourself scarce, alright?"

"Is it all here?" A masculine voice questioned.

"Yes, it's all there." She sounded impatient.

Blu tried to peek around the corner of the building, but she was afraid she'd be spotted. "If you ever breathe a word about this you're going to be in for it, understand?"

"Sure, Kayla. You're so scary." He cleared his throat and Blu didn't miss the sarcastic tone in the man's voice.

Blu stuck her head around the corner just in time to see Kayla disappear around the other side. Whoever she'd given money to was gone as well.

CHAPTER 11

Blu looked around to see if there was anything left behind that would give her a clue as to who the other person might have been that Kayla had been talking to.

"What are you doing back here?"

She looked up to see AJ at the corner of the building. He leaned his shoulder against it. "Shouldn't you be at the memorial?"

Blu felt her heart drop. Was AJ the one that Kayla paid off? What was the money for?

"Shouldn't you?" She held his gaze.

"I was on my way. I heard Kayla stirred up a commotion."

"She did."

"Well, that doesn't tell me what you're doing back here."

"Just walking."

"Funny place to walk."

"Didn't know there were certain places that weren't okay to walk." Blu crossed her arms.

AJ grinned. "Good point. Want to walk back with

me?"

"No, thanks. I've had enough sad music and fake tears."

"Well, maybe you should come to the real memorial. It's tomorrow night at the bar." He tilted his head toward her. "Just do me a favor and don't bring any of the tourists."

"Alright." Blu smiled.

She was sure she could find out a little bit more about Kayla at the real memorial. The only problem was, she wasn't sure if AJ had invited her to be nice, or because he was the person whom Kayla had paid off.

She studied him for a moment. "AJ, have we met before? Before the Beach Bum, I mean?"

"No, I don't think so." He shrugged.

Blu nodded but she couldn't shake the feeling that she knew him somehow. "Thanks for the invite."

"I can see that you cared about Sam."

"I wish I'd had the chance to get to know him better."

"Me too. It's funny—we lived in the same town for so long, but our lives didn't really intersect very often."

"I guess that's just the way it is sometimes. Did you go to school together?"

AJ grinned. "No. I was done with high school before he was close to starting. I'm thirty-two."

Blu's eyes widened. "Wow, you look a lot younger."

"Thanks!" He laughed.

"I'm sorry, I just meant that I didn't think you were close to my age. Sometimes I feel like I'm the oldest person in the world here at the beach. I guess that comes from working with kids and being surrounded by nannies who are much younger."

"Well, I'm here to tell you, Blu, you're not the oldest person in the world. If you ever want to be reminded of that, stop by the bar any time." He turned and started to walk away.

Blu considered stopping him to ask him a few more questions, but she decided against it. She didn't want to risk having her invite revoked.

She walked back toward the memorial at a slow pace. With every step that drew her closer to the gathering, her mind grew more clouded. Sam would be buried soon. From what she understood, the local police didn't think his death was anything more than an accident. Could someone really be murdered and no one ever know? If Sam had been seeing someone else, would that have been enough to drive Kayla to hire someone to murder him?

It made her sick to her stomach to even think about it. Her life was so idyllic that she found it hard to believe that these things even happened. In the small town where she'd grown up, nothing truly tragic ever happened. All of this was a bit much for her to take in.

She took a deep breath and thought about the classes she'd taken in college. The biggest rule of journalism was detachment. She had to be able to keep her distance if she was going to figure all this out. The first step was to go to the police and tell them her suspicions. She wanted to know why the local police were so determined not to investigate Sam's death.

When she reached the chairs, they were already being folded up. The memorial was over.

She glanced around for Maddie, but didn't see her. She did see Brian near the water. His hands were tucked into his pockets and his body seemed relaxed.

Blu reminded herself to have a serious conversation with Maddie. She knew enough about Brian Ross to be certain that he was a womanizer who liked to take advantage of his staff, and she didn't want Maddie to fall into that trap.

As if he sensed her thoughts, Brian turned around to face her. He smiled and raised his hand in a small wave. Blu didn't wave back. She pretended she didn't even notice him.

Chelsea was collecting the remaining flowers from the ribbons.

"What a disaster." She sighed as Blu walked up to her.

"Did you raise a good amount of funds?"

"Sure, but that woman put a real damper on the entire memorial."

"Well, she was his girlfriend. Of course she was upset."

"And that gives her the right to ruin my memorial?" Chelsea shook her head. "I don't think so. I'm going to find out her name and make sure she gets a fine of some kind or something."

"Chelsea, listen to yourself. This woman lost her boyfriend—the man she loved. So she went a little crazy, that's bound to happen."

"Oh, really? If she loved him so much then why did I see her slap him across the face just two days ago? I don't know about you, Blu, but I don't think of that as love."

"She slapped him? You saw this?" Blu piled some flowers into the bin that Chelsea held.

"Yes. I was bringing some things to the dry cleaners and I saw the two of them outside that horrible bar. She looked a little drunk, to be honest. They argued and then out of nowhere she just slapped him really hard across the face. I could hear it from where I was and he even stumbled a little. What kind of person does that?" She clucked her tongue. "Love should never be violent."

Blu frowned as she recalled Kayla's conversation with the man behind the building a few minutes before. She had a pretty good idea about why Kayla was angry with Sam. He broke up with her and may have been cheating on her. But if she was angry enough to hit him, would she be angry enough to hire someone to take revenge for her?

"I have to go." Blu shook her head. "Look, Chelsea— the memorial wasn't a disaster. You helped Sam's family, and that means a lot."

"I hope so." Chelsea scrunched up her nose. "Next time, I'm hiring more security."

CHAPTER 12

Chelsea's mention of security made Blu think of what Shawna had said about the police force in town. Blu hadn't had any run-ins with the police, but she just assumed that they were there if she ever needed them. Were they? She decided to take her concerns straight to the source and find out whether or not Shawna had the right impression.

The afternoon light had begun to fade. Blu started to regret walking instead of driving to the police station. It was only a little further ahead, but the darker it got the more uneasy she became. She was accustomed to living in houses with high-tech security systems. She rarely went out in the evening alone any more. The town was quiet, but there was bound to be activity somewhere.

When she reached the police station, she walked right in. A very large police officer snoozed at the front desk. He snorted and woke himself up when she paused in front of him.

"Oh, hi. Excuse me." He picked up a tissue and wiped at the corner of his mouth. "How can I help you?"

"I'm here to speak to someone about a possible crime."

"A possible crime? Was there a crime or wasn't there?" He opened up a notepad in front of him.

"Well, I think there might have been. But I don't have any proof of it."

His gray eyebrows lifted and his forehead wrinkled. "What do you think might have happened?"

"It's about Sam."

"The lifeguard?"

"Yes."

"Okay. What about him?"

"I just wondered if a thorough investigation was being done involving his death."

"Well, we found his body on the beach, determined that he drowned, and notified his family. Is that thorough enough for you?"

"Did you ever consider that it may not have been an accident?"

"Now why in the world would we ever consider something like that?" The new voice came from an open office door behind the front desk and to the right of where she stood talking to the officer. The man stepped out of the office and crossed over to where Blu stood, extending his hand—looking less than pleased to meet her. "Paul Pitman—Diamond Bay's chief of police."

Blu shook his hand.

"I've heard from a quite few people that there is good

reason to suspect that Sam's death was a result of foul play," she continued before she could think about her words.

"Let me explain something to you, miss. Nothing happens in this town. People don't die, unless it's of old age or sickness. When something like this happens—a handsome young man taken far too early—their imaginations start to run wild. It's as simple as that."

"What if some of their concerns are valid?" Blu frowned. "Have you even considered it?"

"Have I invented a crime where a crime does not exist? No, I haven't." He folded his arms across his chest.

"So it doesn't seem odd to you that Sam, a strong swimmer, an athlete, an experienced lifeguard, would die in calm water? That just seems like poor police work to me."

"Oh, does it?" He chuckled. "What do you do for a living again?"

"I'm a nanny."

"And that makes you an expert on crime fighting?"

"I don't have to be an expert on it to know when it's not being done." Blu's heart pounded as the words slipped out of her mouth. Was she really getting into an argument with the chief of police? That was among the worst ideas she'd ever had.

"Now listen, I'm guessing that you nanny for one of those Hollywood actresses that work on those dramatic police shows, but this is real life. Police resources can't just be wasted looking into a crime that never happened."

"Oh, they're better spent on drool tissues?" Blu shook her head. "I think I might just have to tell the very wealthy engineer that I work for, that this area is not safe because of its poor police force, and that we would be better off selling the beach house and moving on to a new place to spend our summers."

"Are you attempting to threaten me?" He took a step out from behind the front desk. "Is this what you think you can get away with here?"

"I just want Sam's death to be investigated. And I'm not the only one. Obviously his death was suspicious—that's why people are talking about it."

"Do you hear this, Mitch?" He looked over at the sleepy officer behind the desk. "Nanny—" He looked back at her. "What's your name again?"

"Blu."

"Nanny Blu over here wants to tell me how to do my job. Well, I'll tell you what—if you bring me the slightest shred of evidence, any kind of actual proof that Sam's death was not an unfortunate accident, then I will open a case. Until then, I'll be happy to refer you to the library, where they have great true-life crime novels for you to enjoy." He laughed, then turned and sauntered back to his office.

Blu's cheeks burned. She bit into her tongue to keep from saying worse things than she already had. It was clear that Paul Pitman, the chief of police, was not going to take her seriously until she did exactly what she said she'd do. She'd bring him evidence and force him to keep his word about opening an investigation.

This was no longer just about a man who lost his life, but about a police chief who needed a wake-up call.

CHAPTER 13

As Blu stormed out of the police station she nearly collided with Shawna on the sidewalk out front.

"Hey, watch it!" She paused and looked at Blu. "You're that woman from the bar, aren't you?"

"Yes." Blu started to walk past her.

"What were you doing here?"

"I was trying to have a reasonable conversation with the police chief."

"Oh, Uncle Paul?" Shawna laughed. "Good luck with that."

"I don't think it's funny. He was quite rude."

"Don't worry about that. It's just his way. I give him a hard time, but he's actually a decent man. If you give him a chance, he'll show you that his bark is much worse than his bite."

"Maybe so, but he isn't interested in investigating a potential murder."

"Are you talking about Sam?" Shawna's eyes grew wide. "Are you really going to get into the middle of that?"

"Yes. I am." Blu blinked. She wasn't sure how she had ended up in the middle of this, but now she was sure there was only one way out—solving the crime.

"Well, if you need any help let me know. I'd love to see someone brought to justice. Sam didn't deserve to die like that."

Blu nodded. "I may just take you up on that."

She glanced at her watch and realized it was way past dinner. She never stayed out so late—just in case Rachel needed her, even if she was off for the evening.

She hurried back to the beach house to find that it was dark. Rachel had left a note to let her know that she and the kids had gone out to dinner.

Blu sighed as she closed the door to her room. Was she taking too big of a risk by getting in the middle of all this?

That night, as she went to bed, her mind was filled with the events of the day. There was so much to sort out, not the least of which was whether the police force could be trusted.

As she tried to fall asleep, she remembered the sensation of the water rising up along her neck when the little boy she'd helped rescue had tried to pull her down. She remembered the strength of Sam's grip and how he'd swum with such ease.

Blu spent most of her life in the background. She spent her time with someone else's children, acting as a guide and chauffeur. She lived in a home that was not her own and drove a car that was not her own. Now, she was running the risk of stirring up the locals and the wealthy with her focus on Sam's death. And still, Sam could truly have just drowned. It all could have been an accident. Yet every instinct in her body was telling her that it wasn't and that it was worth her digging a bit more.

In the morning Rachel had some news for Blu.

"Marshall is flying in a day early so he can have dinner with the kids and me tonight. He has to meet with some clients so it's going to be a working dinner, but at least they will get some time with their dad."

"Oh, wonderful. I'll get Joey's suit out and the purple dress for Marley…"

"Yes, that would be fine." Rachel was all smiles as she shared breakfast with the kids.

Although Blu was distracted by Sam's death, it was nice to see Rachel excited about her husband's visit. There was nothing that pleased Blu more than seeing the family she worked for happy.

As she washed the dishes from breakfast her mind returned to Sam and the conversation she'd had with Chief Pitman. What kind of evidence *could* she find?

"Kids, why don't we take a walk on the beach this morning to collect some shells? We could use them to make a special gift for your mom and dad."

"If I find a crab, can I keep it?" Joey grinned.

"Only if you promise not to put it in the bathtub."

"Okay." Joey laughed. "I won't do that again."

"I hope not." Blu laughed too. The last time Joey brought a pet home from the beach, his mother found it when she tried to take a bubble bath. It was quite an eventful night for the family.

"Go get dressed and we'll head out. Marley, I put some clothes on your bed to wear."

As the kids ran off Blu pulled out her phone and texted Maddie.

Can you meet at the beach for shell hunting?

Maddie texted back right away.

Sure, we'll be there in 30.

Blu tucked her phone back into her pocket and wondered how her friend would react to what she was going to ask of her. It was risky to take the next step that she'd planned, but she didn't know how else she would get any evidence to prove Sam's death wasn't an accident.

"Ready!" Joey ran past her with a large bucket.

"Me too!" Marley barreled by with her entire collection of sand toys in a big beach bag.

Blu laughed and picked up the shovels and sifters that had fallen out of the bag as Marley ran by. She loved the enthusiasm that children had. To her, they truly understood how to live life, not limited by the concerns and insecurities of adults—a lesson more adults around her could use. Blu couldn't help the thought that often entered her mind.

CHAPTER 14

When they reached the beach Maddie was just pulling up. She only had Chrissa with her.

"Where's Brennan?" Blu waved to Chrissa as she ran off to hunt for crabs with Joey.

"He's asleep. That's what he does now. Sleep and more sleep." Maddie shook her head. "I'm having a hard time connecting with him."

"Just give it time. The older they get, the harder it can be to figure out what's going on in their heads."

"I see that." Maddie sighed. Then she looked at Blu with a furrowed brow. "What's going on with you? You don't look like you've had much sleep."

"I slept, but not well."

"Still thinking about Sam?"

"I had quite an encounter with Chief Pitman last night."

"Why?" Maddie's eyes widened.

"I wanted to know why he hasn't been looking into the possibility of Sam's death not being an accident. He was not very responsive. Basically, he said if I couldn't bring him some kind of evidence, he wouldn't be opening an investigation."

"Wow, so you really think Sam was murdered?" Maddie lowered her voice.

"I think that something isn't right, and it should be looked into. If the people who knew him the best are so sure that he wouldn't have died this way, then why not? But that's not enough for Chief Pitman."

"Oh, Blu." Maddie folded her hands behind her back and turned to watch the kids. "I think you might be getting in too deep."

"Someone has to, right?" Blu pursed her lips. "There was this case I studied when I was in college. It was about a man on death row. Everyone was convinced without question that he was guilty. Everyone but one journalist. That journalist did tons of research, conducted his own investigation, and saved that man's life by proving his innocence."

"But you're not a journalist. You're a nanny." Maddie looked over at her and met her eyes. "And if there's one thing you've taught me about working for the wealthy, it's that they like to keep their private lives private. If you dig around, you're either going to find things you don't like, or you're going to end up without a job."

"I know." Blu frowned. "I'm breaking all my own rules. But I think it's the right thing to do—the only thing that I can do. No one else is looking for justice, and if it falls on me, then it falls on me."

"Who do you think did it?"

"Honestly, I'm not sure. I mean, Kayla seemed pretty angry at him because he broke up with her. But can someone who claims to love someone so much really have him killed?"

"I've always been told there's a fine line between love and hate."

"Do you think you could get me a meeting with Penelope?"

"Hm. Yeah, I think that's possible. You really think she's involved in this somehow?"

"I thought for sure I saw her on the beach the night before Sam died. They were arguing. Everyone's been hinting at Sam hooking up with someone from the summer houses. You mentioned that Penelope seemed to have a new boyfriend. It could easily be Sam. Right?"

"Well, she said she was out of town, but honestly she did get back pretty fast. I guess it's worth looking into. I'll ask her to meet with you."

"Maybe you could suggest the carnival with the kids? I'm taking Joey and Marley tomorrow."

"That would be perfect. I know that she's been needing some family time."

"Great, so I can get a chance to talk to her when we're there. I'll do my best to keep it casual, and I promise not to mention you."

"Sounds like a plan. I just hope that your suspicions

aren't right. I'd hate to think of Penelope involved in anything criminal."

"She has a lot to lose."

"That's for sure."

"Blu! Blu! Look what I got!" Marley's sweet voice called out to her.

Blu spotted her by the foot of the lifeguard stand. Blu jogged over to take a look at what the little girl was holding. Marley proudly displayed something sparkly. It looked like a coin at first. Then, as she took it from Marley's hand, she saw that it was a cufflink. It was engraved with a lion.

"This is an odd thing to find on the beach." She showed it to Maddie.

"Oh, wow." Maddie's eyes widened.

"What is it?"

"I think that might be Brian's."

"Might be?" Blu narrowed her eyes.

"Yes. He was looking for it. He has a pair with lions on it."

"When was he looking for it?"

"He wanted to wear them to the memorial." Maddie bit into her bottom lip. "He ended up not wearing any."

"He must have been the person that was arguing with Sam the night before he died. It was after I left."

"Oh, this is not looking good." Maddie lowered her voice. "Maybe he found out about Penelope and Sam."

"Maybe. But we don't even know for sure yet that

there was a Penelope and Sam."

"That's true."

"I've got to get the kids home for lunch. They're going out to dinner tonight with some of Marshall's clients. Let me know what Penelope says about the carnival."

Maddie nodded. "I will."

"And Maddie, make sure you don't breathe a word about this to either of them. If either one of them is involved, then they're potentially dangerous—as crazy as that sounds around here. Whoever did this will do anything to keep from being found out. I'm pretty sure about that."

"Could you imagine if it's true? How could either of them kill Sam?"

"I don't know. But I'm going to find out the truth, no matter what it takes. Joey, Marley—we have to go!" Blu waved the children over.

As they collected their toys she tucked the cufflink into her pocket. It might not be enough to convince Chief Pitman, but it was a start.

CHAPTER 15

"Blu, I'm so glad you're here."

"What's wrong, Rachel?" Blu surveyed the demolished kitchen.

"I was looking for scissors. I can't find scissors anywhere! I had a thread loose on my dress and I just wanted to snip it off before dinner, and I couldn't find scissors anywhere! Why is that? Shouldn't there be scissors?"

"After Marley snipped her hair at home last month, I always make sure they're above her reach." Blu reached into one of the cabinets above the sink. "I'm sorry. I should have told you where I moved them."

Rachel sniffled and took the scissors.

Blu noticed the way her hands shook when she gripped them. "Rachel, are you okay?"

"I don't know. I feel like a wreck. I'm so nervous about Marshall coming home and not wanting to stay."

"Rachel." Blu hugged her close. "He's going to want to stay. Marshall loves you."

Rachel clung to her. "You're right, I know you're

right. It's just so hard with him gone so long. If I didn't have you around, what would I do?"

"Rachel, you're an amazing mother, and an intelligent, capable woman. You're going to be fine."

"I hope so." Rachel sighed and pulled away from her.

"Why don't you go get a massage? It'll help you relax, and by the time you get back, the kids will be ready for dinner."

"You must think I'm a mess." She shook her head.

"No, I don't think that at all. I think you've done a great job of keeping this family together and you just need a break. Go get a massage, buy a new dress for tonight, and remember how much Marshall loves you."

"Blu, you're amazing." She kissed her cheek. "I want you to know that you really are part of the family and I don't know what we'd do without you."

"Thank you." Blu smiled.

As Rachel left the house, Blu couldn't help but wonder if her employer would still feel that way when she found out about Blu's push for the investigation into Sam's death.

Blu spent the afternoon tidying up and playing cards with the kids. When it was time to get ready for dinner she summoned Joey to his room to put on his suit.

"Are you excited to see your dad?"

"I guess." He shrugged.

"We're going to the carnival tomorrow. We'll have a

great time." She straightened his tie. "Tonight you mind your manners, spend some special time with your dad, and tomorrow we'll go wild. Alright?"

Joey nodded, but he didn't look any happier. "Why do I have to be nice to him, Blu?"

"Joey, he's your father and he loves you."

"But he's never here." Joey frowned.

"Why do you think that is, sweetie?" Blu met his eyes. "What do you think your dad is doing when he's not with you?"

"Working, I guess."

"That's right. He works very hard because he loves you and your mother and your sister. Maybe he doesn't always get to have fun with you, but he does his best to make sure that you have everything you could ever need. That's pretty great, don't you think?"

Joey smiled. "I guess so."

"Make sure you tell him that when you see him. Hm?" She touched her fingertip to his nose.

"I will."

"Good. Now go see if your sister needs help finding her shoes."

Joey ran off down the hall.

Blu heard the front door open and close. "Blu?"

"The kids are just about ready."

"Great, we're going to meet Marshall at the restaurant." Rachel walked further into the kitchen and Blu caught sight of her.

"Oh, you look gorgeous." Blu smiled at her. "I love the new dress."

"Thanks."

"I'll just check on Marley's hair." Blu found Marley with her feet through the sleeves of her dress. "Oops, I think we need to fix that." Blu laughed and helped Marley to get her dress on correctly. Then she tied her bouncy curls back with a purple ribbon. "There you go, sweetheart. You're all set."

Marley hugged her tight and then ran for her mother.

After Blu saw them off she sat down at her computer. She decided to see if she could track down what Brian Ross had been up to lately. Sam was nearly invisible on the Internet, but Brian was the complete opposite. There were pictures of him all over the place. She had just opened one particular website that featured the husbands of powerful wives when there was a knock at the door. Blu rushed toward it.

"Did you forget something?" She opened the door, expecting Rachel to be on the other side.

"No." AJ smiled. "Sorry to intrude."

"What are you doing here?"

"I wanted to talk to you."

Blu's heart raced. "How did you even know where I live?"

"It wasn't hard to find out. Can I come in?" He started to move forward.

"No, I don't think that would be a good idea. I'll

come out." She stepped outside and pulled the door closed behind her. "Now why are you here, AJ?"

"I'm here because I heard what you did today at the police station."

"Of course you did. The police chief is your uncle, right?"

"Yes." He grimaced. "That's not something I like to advertise, though."

"So, are you here to warn me too?"

"No." He met her eyes. "I'm here to offer you my help."

"Why?"

"Sam was a good guy. He didn't deserve this. If he was murdered, then whoever did it should be brought to justice. If you're bold enough to see to that, I can be brave enough to help you."

"I didn't ask for your help."

"I know. I'm here to offer it."

"What do you know?" Blu locked eyes with him.

"Look, it's hard to keep a business afloat here without catering to certain clientele."

"What are you saying?"

"I'm saying that there's more to the Beach Bum than meets the eye."

"I don't understand." Blu raised an eyebrow.

"There's an upstairs. It's only open to the wealthy—it's considered a VIP lounge of sorts." He reached up and rubbed the back of his neck. "All employees have to sign a non-disclosure agreement when they're hired."

CHAPTER 16

Blu smiled at AJ. "So there's an entire hidden bar upstairs? That's intriguing."

"It's not exactly a bar. It's more like a restaurant. Nothing too wild, just a place for the people from the beach houses to unwind without having the riff-raff around."

"Riff-raff?"

"Sure. You know—the help, the lifeguards—all of that."

"Wow. I'm surprised you support that." Blu shook her head.

"I don't exactly. I inherited the bar from my father, and the routine has been established for so long, that it's hard to just shut it down. Besides, it doesn't hurt anybody and the waitresses make great tips."

"Like Kayla? Is she one of the waitresses?"

"How did you know that?"

"She seemed to have a lot of anger toward the summer crowd. I'm guessing she hasn't had the best experiences upstairs."

"No, not the best. People can be cruel when they don't get things exactly the way they want. Kayla was on probation because of a few complaints."

"Did she mess up orders?"

"No, it was nothing like that." He frowned. "That's what I came here to tell you. I could lose the bar over this, so I need to know that you'll be cautious with what I'm sharing with you." He looked into her eyes. "If I lose the bar, I lose everything."

"I'll be careful. I promise." Blu held her breath and waited to find out what AJ had to say.

"Some of the elite crowd like the company of certain people."

"What?"

"I mean, sometimes they see someone they want to spend time with and they make an offer. Then they can spend time with those people upstairs—no questions asked. It's just drinks and meals. What happens after they leave is their business."

"Just cut to the chase, AJ; who are we talking about here?" Blu leveled her gaze on him.

"Sam was a popular request. But he never took the bait. I'd make him the offer, he'd refuse. He just wasn't the type. Plus, he was head over heels in love with Kayla, and he never wanted to do anything to jeopardize that."

"Sweet." Blu smiled a little.

"It was. Until someone made Sam an offer that he

couldn't refuse."

"What do you mean?"

"A particular person really wanted some of his attention. She made a bigger offer than I've ever seen anyone make. I took it to Sam, and he accepted it. All he had to do was spend the evening with her—wine and dine her, so to speak."

"Basically as an escort?"

"Sam was under no obligation. It was more like she offered him a gift, and he did this to say thank you."

Blu rubbed her arms up and down. "That gives me the chills."

"Maybe so, but it's how things have been done around here for a long time."

Blu frowned. "So, who was the woman?"

"I really shouldn't say." AJ grimaced.

"How about if I guess?" Blu narrowed her eyes. "Penelope Ross?"

His eyes widened. "How did you guess that? Did someone tell you?"

"I saw them arguing on the beach the night before Sam was found dead. AJ, do you have any idea what that argument might have been about?"

"Well, all I know for sure is that Sam took the money from her. He showed up, he wined and dined her, and then when she asked him to go home with her, he refused. She was furious. He offered to give her all of her money back. She shouted back that it wasn't about the money and he knew that. She was—get this"—AJ lowered his voice—"In love with him. Can you believe it?"

Blu shook her head. "So Penelope fell in love, but Sam didn't feel the same way about her. She must have tried again that night. Did Sam give her the money back?"

"I don't know. After she left that night, I didn't see her again. I'm only telling you this because I thought it might help your investigation."

"I guess it will. Do you think Sam broke up with Kayla to be with Penelope?"

AJ shoved his hands deep down into his pockets. "He was in love with Kayla. I don't think that's something that you can just turn off."

"But he did break up with her." Blu began to pace in front of the door. "He has almost no money, his parents lose their home, then Penelope swoops in with this grand offer. He can't resist taking the money. It will change his life, change his parents' life. All for dinner and drinks?"

"He probably broke things off with Kayla because he didn't want to cheat on her. Maybe he figured that if he took the money it would bother her."

"Or maybe he told her about it. Maybe Kayla was the one who broke things off."

"She's told everyone who will listen that he broke up with her."

"Hm." Blu tapped her fingers lightly against the exterior wall of the house. "I think I need to have a talk with Kayla."

"Good luck. She's off the rails. No one's seen her since the memorial."

His comment reminded her of the last time that she'd seen Kayla. "Does that include you?"

"What do you mean?" AJ leaned against the wall beside her.

"I mean, what were you doing on the beach behind the restrooms?"

"Uh, am I under investigation now?" He chuckled. "Should you be?"

"Really? After I came all the way over here and told you what I know—told you things that could risk everything I own?"

"Really." Blu set her jaw. "Why would you tell me those things? You're the man who runs a bar that has a secret upstairs for the elite—the man who looks the other way as people in his town are essentially employed as escorts. You're the man whose uncle, the police chief, refuses to open an investigation into this crime. So why all of a sudden would you grow a conscience?"

"You think you're pretty smart." He lifted an eyebrow and held her gaze. "Have me all figured out, do you?"

"Maybe. So why were you there?"

"You tell me."

Blu studied him. "Are you here to help me or not, AJ?"

"I am."

"Then why were you on the beach?"

"I was there to see Kayla."

"So you were the one she paid off?"

He cleared his throat. "It's not what you think."

"Then what was it?"

"It's personal."

"If you want me to believe you, you need to tell me the truth."

"The truth isn't yours to know. I'm willing to help—if there's a way I can."

"Maybe there is. You could get me into the elite section of that special little club of yours."

AJ raked his eyes over her loose khakis and sleeveless top. "You're going to have to change."

"I can do that."

"Alright. I'll wait out here for you."

CHAPTER 17

Blu closed the door and locked it behind her. Once inside she caught her breath. She couldn't get a straight answer out of AJ and she wasn't sure what to think about it. One minute he seemed helpful, the next, evasive and certainly not trustworthy.

Blu tended to trust far too easily. She'd never been deceived by anyone before. Now it seemed as if she was being lied to by everyone she met. She ran into her room and looked through her closet. She only had her summer wardrobe at the beach house—nothing that would fit in at this so-called elite club.

She left her room and stepped into Rachel's. As a rule of thumb she never entered her employer's bedroom unless there was a good reason to. Borrowing clothes was not a good reason, but it was her only option.

She found a sleek black cocktail dress. When she pulled it on, it was skin-tight and uncomfortable. She looked in the mirror and decided it would do, but it looked very plain. She grabbed a scarf to toss around her shoulders and pinned her hair up in a messy bun.

When she stepped out through the door, AJ took a slight step back.

"Wow."

"I'm not looking for compliments." She did her best to hide a smile.

"I can't help it. I didn't expect you to—uh—to look like that."

Blu quirked her eyebrow. "Okay…"

"But as beautiful as you look, I don't think those shoes are going to work." He looked down at her feet.

Blu looked down as well. Only then did she realize that she was still in flip-flops.

"Oops. One more second." She ducked into the house and stepped back out in heels.

"That's better." He nodded. "I'll drive you over."

"I can walk." She started to take a step forward, but the heel of her shoe caught in the welcome mat in front of the door. Her ankle twisted and she had to grab on to AJ's arm to keep from falling over.

"Not in those you can't." He smiled and tucked her arm under his.

Blu couldn't exactly argue that point. She leaned on him for support as he led her to his car. When he opened the door for her, she hesitated. Was it safe to get in?

"What? Do you want to drive?" He grinned.

Something about AJ's boyish expression disarmed her.

She shook her head and settled into the passenger seat. The short drive to the Beach Bum was awkward. Blu did her best to keep her eyes on the window. AJ didn't attempt to make conversation.

Once they parked she opened her door before he could even turn off the car. She stepped out and started toward the front door of the bar.

"Not that way." He steered her away from the front door and walked her around to the back. He pointed out a set of stairs that was nearly hidden from view by an extension of the building. "This is the VIP entrance."

"I have to climb in these?" Blu looked down at her high heels with concern.

"Don't worry, I'll be right behind you."

"For some reason that doesn't make me feel better." Blu fixed her eyes on his for a moment, then turned and walked up the stairs.

At the top, AJ reached past her to open the door. "Remember, don't breathe a word about who you are."

"I won't forget." Blu tugged at the skirt of the dress. She wasn't handling how tight it was very well.

AJ led her into the main area of the lounge. It was set up more as a casual living room than a bar—with overstuffed chairs, small tables, and a few flat screens hanging on the walls. It wasn't what she'd expected it to be.

AJ took position behind the bar and Blu settled onto a bar stool after wrestling a bit with her dress. It wasn't easy for her to sit in something so short. She couldn't imagine how Rachel did it so effortlessly.

As AJ delivered her a drink she was very aware that there were eyes on her.

She returned the favor by surveying everyone in the room. One of the first people that she noticed was a tall man who sat at a table by himself. He had a bottle of beer in front of him, but his attention seemed to be focused on the people rather than the drink. She saw him gesture to AJ.

CHAPTER 18

When AJ walked over, the man leaned close to him.

Blu was close enough that she could still make out the conversation.

"Is Penelope coming in tonight?"

"I haven't seen her."

"It's been a while."

"I know. I think with Sam's death—"

"Yes." The man nodded. "I understand." He sighed and finished his drink. As he stood up from the table he pulled out his cell phone, holding it to his ear as he walked toward the stairs. As he passed by Blu's table he held the phone away from his ear to hang it up, but not before Blu heard Penelope's voice recorded on a voicemail.

She had assumed all along that Sam was Penelope's boyfriend. What if she was wrong?

She decided to follow after the man. When she hit the top of the stairs she got one of her shoes caught in the metal bars. She could see the man walking toward a car.

With a growl of frustration she snatched her shoes off. She hurried down the steps with her shoes dangling from one hand. She didn't think she would be able to catch up with him, but she had to try.

When she'd reached the bottom of the stairs she almost ran directly into someone who was just on their way up.

"I'm sorry." She kept her head down but stole a glance at the person. When she saw who it was it sent a shock through her senses.

Brian Ross.

"Blu?" He offered an easy smile. "I didn't know you were part of all this."

"I'm not."

"No? Shame." He shrugged. "I'd invite you upstairs for a drink, but it seems that you're on your way out."

"I am." She paused.

As much as it disgusted her to be thought of as part of the elite club, it intrigued her that Brian was there and that he was unafraid of inviting her up for a drink. It obviously wasn't his first time.

If Penelope met Sam here, was it possible that Brian had found out? Maybe he'd caught the two together. He was a massive, muscular man, and could have easily held Sam under the water. It made more sense to her than the idea of petite Kayla doing it.

Then of course, there was always AJ, who was muscular himself and likely more than capable of pinning

Sam down. He had also received some kind of payment from Kayla.

When it came to Sam's death, the issue wasn't so much that there were no suspects as it was that there were multiple people who likely wanted him dead and were capable of making that happen.

If she wanted to rule Brian in or out of the suspect list, then sharing a drink might be the best way to do it.

"Actually, I can spare a few minutes." Blu ducked her head to hide her blush. She was already intimidated by Brian, and now she was putting herself into some kind of awkward position with him. She really hoped that it was going to pay off.

"Wonderful." He took her arm at the crook of her elbow and led her back up the stairs.

When the two of them entered the bar, AJ looked up. His expression grew dark the moment he recognized the pair.

"AJ, can we get a table?" Brian draped his arm casually around Blu's shoulders.

Blu had to bite into the side of her cheek to keep from gagging and squirming out from under him. This is for Sam, she reminded herself.

"Uh, we'll be closing up soon." AJ narrowed his eyes as he walked toward them.

"Relax, AJ, just a couple of drinks."

"Okay." His jaw rippled but he led them to a table and two chairs, then lingered to take their order.

"The lady will have a white wine."

Blu didn't protest. She crossed her legs and folded her hands in her lap. She had no idea how to appear casual when she was so twisted up inside.

Brian looked back at her and smiled. "I'm glad that you decided to stay for a drink."

"Well, I was curious about how things are going with Maddie."

"Oh yes, you were the one that recommended her to us, weren't you?" He accepted his drink from AJ and handed Blu hers.

AJ lingered for a moment longer than he should have but Blu refused to look in his direction.

"Yes, I was."

"She's alright, I suppose. I mean—as nannies go."

"You seem to enjoy her company."

Brian smiled over the rim of his glass. "You noticed?"

"It's hard not to."

"Well, a man can't be blamed for trying, can he?" He swallowed down the liquid in one gulp.

"I don't know. What is your wife's opinion?"

"Is that what this is all about?" He chuckled. "You think that I'm being disloyal to Penelope? How quaint." Blu stared at him.

"I'm sure she doesn't enjoy you putting your arm around her nanny."

"I'm sure she doesn't care." He set his glass down on the table. "Penelope and I have an arrangement. It's a personal thing, but it's an arrangement that works for us. We both enjoy being with other people. So, as we please, we take other lovers. Have you never heard of that before?"

"Well, I—"

"I suppose not. You've never been married, have you, Blu?"

"No." She frowned.

"Well, then you can't know how impossibly boring it can be to wake up next to the same person every day. I mean really—is it even possible that people do that? Penelope and I appreciate having others in our lives, so that we can, in turn, appreciate one another more—it keeps things interesting."

"Was Sam one of the men that Penelope was *appreciating*?" Blu leaned forward in her chair. "Were you aware that your wife offered him money?"

"Listen." Brian narrowed his eyes and balled one hand into a fist, which he smacked into the palm of his other hand as he spoke. "Penelope and I have a very good reputation to uphold. She is well-known and well-respected, not just in this country, but in other countries as well. She has to be careful who knows what, and it makes it much easier to ensure silence if an agreement can be made prior to an encounter. If that agreement involves money or lavish gifts, that's her business."

"I see." Blu sipped her wine.

CHAPTER 19

Blu's mind reeled with the information that Brian was feeding her. Was it true? Was he making it all up? She looked at him carefully. "And what if someone were to find out the truth?"

"That can't happen. That won't happen." His eyes hardened as he looked into hers. "People don't understand our lifestyle—not just friends and family, but business partners. It would ruin Penelope if it got out."

"So then, you two must have been pretty careful."

"Always."

"Did she have a lot of special friends?"

He smiled. "The truth is, I'm the one that takes advantage of our little arrangement a lot more often than she does."

"So, it was only Sam?"

"Look. There's a lot of people involved in all of this. It's easier not to keep track."

"And you never felt jealous?"

"Sure, sometimes. That's part of the fun. It heats things up between the two of us now and then."

"So why were you arguing with Sam on the beach the night before he died?"

Brian tilted his head and looked into her eyes. "You know, Blu, you ask a lot of questions. I think I've had enough to drink."

"Brian, wait—if you weren't jealous, why were you arguing with Sam?"

"I don't have to answer that. I wasn't even on the beach that night."

"I found your cufflink."

"That doesn't prove anything. If it did, I'm sure that you'd be having a conversation with Chief Pitman instead of me." He stood up from the table. "I'd appreciate it if you kept what I told you to yourself. I wouldn't want Rachel and Marshall finding out about how you spend your free time, Blu. If you mention our little conversation to anyone, I'll have to mention that you were here. Understand?"

Blu nodded as she looked up at him. "I understand."

"Stay out of my business." He tossed a twenty down on the table to cover their drinks. "If I want your company again, I'll let you know."

Blu shuddered at the thought.

As soon as Brian was gone, AJ walked up to her.

"What were you thinking, having a drink with Brian Ross? Now everyone is going to know that you were here."

"I don't think so. I don't think that he's going to tell."

"Why not?"

"Because I think he's the one who killed Sam, and I think he will do anything to keep people's attention off of him."

"You think Brian did it? Why?"

"Give me a ride home, and I'll fill you in."

By the time AJ dropped her off, Blu had spilled everything she knew about Sam's death—everything except overhearing a conversation between Kayla and a man on the beach at the memorial. She wasn't convinced just yet that that man wasn't AJ, since he'd come out of nowhere right after the conversation had taken place.

AJ parked in the driveway and stared out through the window. "That's a lot to take in."

"Yes, it is."

"So you think Brian is behind it?"

"I think he could be. Jealousy is a strong motive."

"That it is." He blew some air past his lips. "That's why it's always better to be single."

"I can agree with that." Blu grinned. She opened the door and stepped out of the car. "I'll let you know if I find anything else out.

"Yes, please do that." He cringed. "When I started to help you, I really thought that Sam's death was an accident. But the more you uncover, the less likely that seems."

"I don't think it was an accident. I'm ready to believe

that someone did this to him. The only problem is that there doesn't seem to be a way to prove it.

"There's no evidence on his body of assault, although no one was really looking for it. There's no evidence of someone else being with him at the time of his death. Maybe if the police were willing to investigate, it would be different, but I certainly don't have the forensic knowledge to be able to determine anything from the body. The ocean will have washed anything usable away anyway."

She shook her head and glanced toward the empty driveway. Rachel and Marshall still weren't back from dinner. She hoped that it was a sign that they were having a nice time. "I need to get out of this ridiculous outfit before the family gets back."

"It's not ridiculous." AJ looked at her through the open car window. "Not at all."

Blu caught his eye, then walked up the driveway. She did her best to walk properly, since she was sure that AJ was still watching her.

When she reached the partition between the driveway and the front door her heel slipped and her ankle twisted. She caught herself on the railing that led up the three steps to the front door. As she lost her balance, the railing sunk into the palm of her hand. For a moment she felt dizzy. It reminded her of the sensation of sinking under the water right before Sam had rescued her and the young boy.

Her thoughts shifted back to that moment and the way she was pulled against his body. She imagined seeing something in the water—a boat in the distance.

"That's it!" Her eyes widened. "If the water was so calm that morning, there had to be other people out taking advantage of it."

She rushed inside the house, no longer bothered if AJ had seen her trip. What she needed, to prove that Sam's death was suspicious, was an eyewitness to say that Sam hadn't been alone that morning.

CHAPTER 20

Blu had barely changed out of Rachel's dress before she heard the front door open and close. The lack of little feet running across the floor told her that the kids must already be asleep.

She stuck her head out of her bedroom door and saw Marshall with Joey draped over his shoulder. He smiled at Blu and put his finger to his lips.

Behind him Rachel stepped through the door with Marley in her arms. Rachel winked at Blu. "They tired out not long after dinner. I think they'll stay asleep for the night."

"That's good. They'll need their rest for the carnival."

"You're still okay with us taking off together tomorrow?"

"Absolutely. Do something fun, okay?"

"Thanks, Blu." She smiled over the top of Marley's head and continued down the hall.

Blu closed the door to her room and sat down with her computer. She began researching local boat groups and where she could find the information about who was on the water on the morning of Sam's death. Once she had the information she needed, she took a quick shower and headed to bed.

With every step she took it seemed she was getting deeper into a situation that she might not be able to find her way out of, but it was too late to turn back now. Sam needed someone to fight for him. It looked like she was going to be that person.

In the morning Blu woke to the children climbing into her bed.

"Mom and Dad aren't here." Marley stuck her nose in front of Blu's. "Where are they?"

"They're off on a little mommy and daddy trip."

"Aw." Joey frowned.

"Don't worry, we're going to have a little Nanny Blu, Joey, and Marley trip. We're going to go see some boats this morning and then we're going to a carnival tonight! Won't that be fun?"

"Yes!" Joey jumped up and down on her bed. "I can't wait!"

"Good. Go get dressed and I'll get some breakfast ready."

As the two ran off Blu climbed out of bed. She wasn't quite sure how she was going to juggle the two kids and her investigation, but she'd have to find a way to make it work.

Blu took the kids along with her to the harbor. She pointed out the sailboats, the ferryboats, and the large fishing boats, as if that was the purpose of their visit. Then she took them inside the office so that they could see how everything worked.

"Good morning." She smiled at the woman behind the front desk.

"Good morning." She wiggled her fingers to greet the children. "How can I help you today?"

"Well, I have two very curious children with me. I was wondering if you could explain to them how boaters remain safe on the water? I mean, is there a system in place where a boater will call in to let the harbor master know if they are out on the water?"

"Oh yes, we have both an electronic and verbal system in place."

"Could you perhaps give us an example?" She offered the date that Sam died. "Could you tell us what boats were on the water that morning?"

"Sure; that was a very busy morning because it was very good weather." She typed on her keyboard and then spun the monitor around to show the kids the screen. "It's a bit like a game we old people used to play—where we would position our little boats on a grid of pretend water. Only this grid is real water. So each of these little dots represent a boat that is out on the water. Of course there may be more that didn't report in, but those that do report get a little dot on this grid. We can use a device on their boats called a beacon, to see where the boat is going on the water."

"Wow! Can you see spy boats too?"

"And subs?" Joey and Marley peered at the screen.

"I can't say for sure that I've ever seen a spy boat or a submarine, but I have seen plenty of sailboats."

"And what kind of information do you record?" Blu leaned closer. "Like this boat here." She pointed at the boat on the screen closest to the area where Sam died. "Are you able to tell what kind of boat that is and who owns it?"

"It depends on how accurate and up-to-date the information is that the owner of the boat has sent us, but usually yes. See, if I click on this dot it will pull up the name of the owner, their address, the registration number of the vessel, and the type of boat it is. This particular one is owned by Jeffery Miles and it's a sailboat. Jeffery—I think—is only about eighteen. He was in one of our young sailor classes, and we teach all of our kids to always report in to the harbor master in case they run into any trouble on the water."

"Wow, this is very impressive. Isn't it, kids?" She memorized the address on the screen before the woman turned it back around to face her.

"Yes! I want to be a young sailor!"

"There are still some openings in the summer program." The woman smiled.

"Please, Blu? Please can I do it?"

"Well, we'll have to check with your parents first, Joey." Blu patted the top of his head. She could imagine the amount of pleading that would happen before Rachel would finally give in. "Thanks for your time." She nodded to the woman and led the kids out of the office.

As they walked toward the car, she typed the address for Jeffery Miles into her phone. It was on the south end of town and would only take about five minutes to get to.

"Alright, guys, we're going to make a quick stop before lunch."

CHAPTER 21

Blu drove to the house, which was directly on the water. It was small and the paint was peeling on the front of it.

As she stepped out of the car, a large brown dog charged toward her. Her heart jolted with fear as the dog jumped up into the air with a loud snarl.

"Duke, no!" A voice came from the side of the house, and a young man appeared in Blu's line of vision a second later.

Blu was knocked to the ground by the force of the large dog's paws striking her shoulders. She winced and tried to shield her face from the dog's mouth. The dog nuzzled his way past her hands and began to lick her cheeks, forehead, and even the tip of her nose.

"Aw!" Joey giggled as he stuck his head out of the car window. "He likes you, Blu!"

"I'm so sorry." The young man, whom she assumed to be Jeffery, tugged the dog off Blu. "He really enjoys having visitors."

Blu managed to get to her feet just as Joey and Marley

slipped out of the car.

"Careful, kids." She frowned.

"I promise, he's really very gentle." Jeffery crouched down beside the dog and stroked his neck. "You guys want to pet him?"

"Sure." Joey smiled and began stroking the dog's fur. Marley hid behind Blu's leg, still unsure.

"Are you Jeffery?" Blu met his eyes.

"Yes."

"My name is Blu, and these are the children I nanny for—Joey and Marley."

"Nice to meet you all." Jeffery squinted up at her. "Is there something I can help you with?"

"Actually, yes. I wanted to know if you were out sailing on the morning that Sam—the lifeguard—had his accident?"

Jeffery's face drained of color. "How did you know that?"

"I checked with the harbor master."

"Well, yeah. I was out on the water that morning."

"You seemed to be pretty close to the area where Sam ran into trouble."

Jeffery glanced away and frowned. "Maybe."

"Jeffery, I'm not here to cause you any trouble. I just want to know if you saw anything—out of the ordinary, I mean."

"I didn't see anything." Jeffery shook his head.

Marley dared to step out from behind Blu's leg,

reaching down to pet the dog too.

"Are you sure? Maybe it didn't seem important at the time," Blu continued.

"I didn't see anything." Jeffery gritted his teeth.

"I guess that you knew Sam pretty well, hm?" Blu raised an eyebrow. "He probably helped with the young sailor's club?"

Jeffery lowered his eyes. "Yes, he did."

"I'm sorry for your loss."

Jeffery swallowed hard. "Me too."

"You were the only one close enough to see anything—if there was anything to see. You don't have to be afraid to tell me the truth, Jeffery."

He looked up and met her eyes. "I wasn't even supposed to be out on the water. I was grounded. I snuck out in the morning because I thought I could get out and back before my dad found out."

"Is that why you didn't tell anyone what you saw?"

"Look, I'm not even sure about what I saw." He picked up a tennis ball and tossed it across the front yard. "Go on, Duke, show the kids how well you fetch." The dog and the children chased after the ball.

"Did you see Sam out surfing that morning?"

"Yes. I waved to him. He waved to me. Then I got a little ways away from him. I turned back to look to see if he caught a solid wave, and I saw him paddling toward the shore."

"He was by himself?"

"Yes." Jeffery narrowed his eyes. "But there was someone on the beach—waiting for him, it seemed."

"Who was it?"

"I was too far out to see him clearly, but he was a big guy—thick, you know?"

"Muscular?"

"Yeah."

"Could you see his face or how he was dressed?"

"He was wearing a windbreaker. I couldn't see his face, though. I was too far out."

"What happened then?"

"Well, I thought it was a little odd for Sam to be going in so soon. He only got to about a few feet out from the shore when the man on the beach started walking into the water. I thought that was strange because the guy wasn't wearing a swimsuit or anything. He had on pants."

"What else did you see?" Blu met his eyes directly. "Did you see them argue?"

Jeffery hung his head. "I was worried about getting back in time, so I started to sail back home. I didn't see anything else. I didn't see them argue or anything."

Blu sighed. "Are you sure, Jeffery?"

"Yeah, I'm sure. Ever since Sam died, it's all I've been thinking about. What if I'd stayed a little bit longer? What if I'd made sure that he got to the shore? Or asked him for some tips? Would he still be alive?"

Blu smiled sympathetically at the young man. He was

barely more than a kid, with a big burden on his shoulders.

"It wasn't your fault, Jeffery, but if you're willing, I'd really like to tell Chief Pitman about what you saw."

Jeffery sighed heavily. "I guess my dad will find out I was out on the water when I wasn't supposed to be."

"He may." Blu nodded.

He shrugged. "I guess if it can help Sam somehow, it's worth it."

"Thanks, Jeffery." Blu rubbed his shoulder. "You're doing the right thing."

Once she pried the kids away from the dog, she herded them into the car with promises of taking them out to lunch. On the way to the restaurant, Blu considered her options. She felt she had a strong enough case to be able to start an investigation.

She settled the kids with their favorite lunch at the restaurant patio, then she dialed the police department.

"May I speak with Chief Pitman, please? It's Blu Parker."

"The chief is in a meeting, may I take a message?"

"Are you sure he's in a meeting or do you think it's possible he's avoiding my call?"

"Ma'am, did you have a message that you wanted to leave?"

"Yes, actually. Please tell Chief Pitman that I have the evidence he requested and that time is of the essence."

She hung up the phone and frowned. Was he going to

go back on his word? Had she done all of this work for nothing?

CHAPTER 22

Just as Blu and the kids were finishing their lunch, a police car pulled up beside the patio. The driver flicked the lights and siren on for the kids to enjoy for a moment. Then he stepped out of the car. Blu was surprised to see that it was Chief Pitman himself.

"Hi, kids." He tipped his hat at the children. "Are you eating your vegetables?"

Joey plucked a carrot up with his fork and put it in his mouth very fast.

Marley stuck out her tongue. "Yuck! No way!" She shook her head.

Chief Pitman laughed. He looked over at Blu. "Well, you have my attention. What evidence did you find?"

Blu stood up from the table and drew him a few steps away from it. "I have a witness that saw Sam in the water with another man that morning. I have evidence that Brian Ross was on that beach."

"Wait a minute, you have a witness that saw Brian Ross with Sam in the water that morning?"

"Uh, no, not exactly. I found Brian Ross' cufflink on the beach, and I have a witness that saw a man fitting his description on the beach that morning with Sam."

"Oh? Your witness identified him as Brian Ross?"

Blu's heart pounded hard. Every time the chief spoke her evidence sounded thinner. She didn't know how to make it sound better.

"Look, I know that Sam was involved with Brian's wife, and that Brian had an argument with him the night before. I know that my witness can prove that Sam was not alone that morning."

"Your witness that never came forward in the first place?" The chief narrowed his eyes. "Is he credible?"

"He was afraid of getting in trouble. He was grounded at the time."

"Oh, great. Well, that's important." Chief Pitman rolled his eyes. "At least tell me that this witness overheard the two arguing or something?"

"No, he was on a sailboat—too far away for him to hear anything that was being said."

"Okay, let me see if I've got everything. Your witness is a scared kid on a sailboat—too far away to see or hear anything of value. And your proof is the fact that some rich woman from the beach house had been running around with Sam? Are you kidding? I'm missing out on my lunch hour for this? Blu, I don't know what you're used to in the city, but around here the police force isn't big enough to waste time on petty theories and the imagination of a bored nanny."

Blu bit the tip of her tongue. She knew that flying off the handle would do nothing to help her case. As difficult as it was for her to face, Chief Pitman was right. She had no solid evidence—nothing that couldn't be explained away or dismissed. It dawned on her in that moment that the only way she was going to prove that Sam had been murdered would be to get the murderer to confess.

"I'm sorry for wasting your time."

Chief Pitman adjusted his hat. "Listen, it's not as if I don't appreciate the effort you're making. You've got real determination. But I think you're trying to see something that just isn't there."

"Or is it just something that you'd prefer not to see? I imagine a local being murdered by someone from the beach house would cause an awful lot of paperwork."

"You need to watch your tone with me." He stuck his finger close to her nose. "I've been very patient with you, Blu, but I promise you, if you step one foot out of line I will show you just how much paperwork I'm perfectly content to fill out. Don't accuse me of covering up anything. Understand?"

Blu took a slight step back.

"Blu? Are you going to jail?" Joey looked at her with wide eyes and a mouthful of grilled cheese.

Blu wasn't sure how to answer that question. With the way Chief Pitman glared at her, she wondered if she might be.

Chief Pitman cracked a smile. "Don't worry, son. Your nanny is doing a great job. Just keep eating those vegetables, hm?"

Joey nodded, but his eyes were still wide. Marley looked up from the tower she'd built with her French fries.

"No way! Yuck!"

"Marley!" Blu raised an eyebrow.

"Cute kids." Chief Pitman grinned, then got into the patrol car and drove off.

Blu's stomach sank as she heard the engine grow more distant. She really was alone in all of this.

After lunch Blu took the kids back to the beach house to get ready for the carnival.

She knew that Maddie had promised to try to get Penelope there. If she could get Penelope to confess to being involved with Sam, that would help bolster the case against Brian. Just as she was having the thought, another one hit her, causing a wave of dread.

Brian wasn't the only person that fit the description that Jeffery had given her. AJ was a very large and muscular man as well.

The first chance she had, she'd ask Maddie to check Brian's closet for a windbreaker. If she had the opportunity she'd get herself invited into AJ's house so that she could search for a windbreaker there. Even if having a windbreaker was fairly common, she might be able to find some evidence on it that could implicate one of the men or at least validate her own suspicions.

CHAPTER 23

When they arrived at the carnival, Blu began looking for Maddie and Penelope. She kept track of the children amidst the crowd, but she was also busy scanning the faces.

"I want to go on the roller coaster!"

"I want to go on the flying planes!"

"Don't worry, we'll get to everything. But first, why don't we get some cotton candy?"

"Yes!" Joey and Marley both shouted.

Blu laughed and walked with them toward a vendor. As she stood in line with the kids, she looked around at the crowd again. The line was long so Blu pulled out her phone and texted Maddie.

We're at the carnival. Are you here?

A second later she received a text back.

Just leaving the parking lot. We're going to the go-karts. Meet there?

Blu sent a text back agreeing to meet her. The line for the cotton candy hadn't budged. She rose up on her toes and tried to look past all the people that stood in front of her.

"Kids, how about we start with something else?"

"No cotton candy?" Marley's bottom lip began to quiver. Her big blue eyes squinted up at Blu. "I want it so bad!"

"I know you do, and we'll still get some. But I want to see what else there is to do. Okay?"

"Okay." Marley sighed.

Blu led the kids over to the area where the go-karts were. Neither was tall enough to ride on one, so they were both impatient about being there. Blu scanned the crowd again.

"Blu!" Maddie waved to her from the gate beside the go-kart course.

"Hi." Blu walked over to her, tugging the kids along with her. "Is Penelope here too?"

"Yes." Maddie lowered her voice. "I sent her to get some cotton candy so you could catch her alone. She's still in a pretty bad mood."

"I imagine she is." Blu narrowed her eyes.

"What?" Maddie raised her voice over the revving engine of a go-kart.

"Do you mind keeping an eye on Joey and Marley for a few minutes while I go talk to her?"

"Sure, it's fine. Mine are on the go-karts anyway. They'll probably be on them all night."

"Thanks."

Blu crouched down in front of Marley. "You stay

here with Maddie, I'm going to go get us our cotton candy, alright?"

"I can watch the cars?"

"Sure you can." Blu ruffled her hair. "Joey, keep on eye on Marley, alright? Make sure she doesn't wander off."

"I'll try." Joey grinned. He grabbed Marley's hand.

Blu walked off toward the cotton candy vendor.

It wasn't hard to spot Penelope. She stood out, even in a t-shirt and jeans. Also, people tended to automatically give her a little space, perhaps because of who she was.

She paused a moment and studied her. Was Brian right? If the society they were a part of got wind of their arrangement, would they turn against the couple?

Blu slipped into line behind Penelope.

Within a few moments Penelope glanced over her shoulder. "Hi, Blu." She smiled a little. "Did you bring the kids?"

"Yes. I left them with Maddie so they wouldn't have to be in this long line."

"Good plan. This line is crazy. I don't want to wait any more."

"Me either. I'll walk back with you?"

"Sure." Penelope nodded and began to walk back toward the go-karts. Blu fell into step beside her.

"I wanted to tell you how sorry I am about Sam."

"Oh? Yes, that was terrible."

"I mean, I know how much you cared about him."

Blu braced herself for the woman's reaction to her words.

"What?" Penelope stopped in the middle of the walkway. "What did you just say to me?"

"Penelope, I don't mean to be intrusive. I just feel awful, knowing how much you liked him—that he was killed."

"Wait a minute!" Penelope glared at her. "What are you talking about? Why would I care about a lifeguard, and what do you mean he was killed? It was an accident."

Blu met her eyes. She remembered Brian's insistence that he and Penelope would do anything to protect their reputation. Was she putting herself in danger by revealing what she knew to Penelope?

"I know about you and Sam. You don't have to worry. I won't breathe a word of it to anyone else. But you should know that it wasn't an accident. Someone killed him."

"That's absurd."

"Is it? You must have admired him for a long time. I'm sure you knew what a strong swimmer he was."

Penelope fell silent. Blu noticed that she didn't attempt to deny the affair.

The Ferris wheel lit up right behind them. As it began to spin the lights swirled and flashed, which created a strobing light effect. Penelope's face shifted from shadowed to garishly lit up.

"What are you implying, Blu?" She stared hard, her rouged lips pressed tight together.

"I'm not judging you, Penelope. I just want to know. If you cared as much about Sam as I think you did, then I would think you'd want to know if your husband had a hand in his death."

"You're accusing my husband of murder?" Her eyes widened, her long lashes defined by the flicker of light. "You're accusing me of infidelity?"

"Am I wrong?" Blu searched her eyes. "Did you know that your husband had an argument with Sam on the beach after you left? That he'd found out about the two of you being together?"

CHAPTER 24

Penelope threw her head back and laughed.

Blu's lips parted with shock at the woman's reaction.

When Penelope's laughter subsided she spoke with a slight giggle. "My husband and I know everything that the other does, Blu. We have an arrangement."

Blu raised an eyebrow. "So Brian was telling me the truth when I spoke to him last night."

"You were with Brian last night?"

"Sure. At the club upstairs—at the Beach Bum."

"Oh?" Penelope cleared her throat. "I didn't think that was the type of place where you'd spend your time."

"It isn't normally. But after I found your husband's cufflink on the beach, I was curious. So when he invited me for a drink, I accepted."

"Just a drink?"

"Didn't he tell you?" Blu tilted her head to the side. "I thought you two told each other everything?"

"Careful, Blu."

"If he didn't tell you about our meeting, what else isn't he telling you, Penelope? What else might he be keeping from you? Perhaps he's not as accepting of your activities as you think. Maybe he thought you were a little too interested in Sam."

'That's nonsense. It's impossible."

"Why? You couldn't imagine your husband being jealous of a man that you were sleeping with?"

"No. And if you must know, Sam and I didn't sleep together."

"But I thought—"

"Yes, you thought you knew everything, didn't you? But no, he turned me down. I offered him an embarrassing amount of money, he accepted, but when it came down to it, he refused. He rejected me." She lowered her eyes. "I guess I really am getting old."

Blu narrowed her eyes. "I find that hard to believe. Why would he reject you?"

"He said he just couldn't live with himself if he did it. Can you believe that? The man had nothing but the sand between his toes, and he couldn't live with the idea of spending one night with me. That's what we were arguing about on the beach. That's what you saw. I was upset because he turned me down."

"Upset enough to send your husband to bully him? They argued over him keeping the money?"

"No, that's not it at all. I hadn't given him the money yet. I hadn't even taken it out of the bank. I wanted him to agree first, and obviously, he didn't. I gave up. He was too much of a boy scout, or he just wasn't attracted to me. Either way, I wasn't about to beg. So I left. I went back home. I never even breathed a word about it to Brian."

"I think you're lying to me. I think you went to Brian, you demanded that he find a way to convince Sam to take your offer, and Brian went back to the beach that night to talk to him about it. Things got out of hand and Brian killed him."

"You're really twisted, Blu, you know that?" Penelope glared at her. "You don't know anything. Brian would never risk something like that. He knows that it would ruin our reputation. Nothing matters to either of us more than our reputation. That's how we've gotten as far as we have. We're a team, and he wouldn't do anything to ruin that."

"Are you sure about that?" Blu searched Penelope's eyes. "People can surprise you sometimes."

Penelope's glare faltered. For a split-second Blu witnessed a glimmer of doubt.

Then Penelope shook her head. "Brian knows how good he has it with me. If you try to cause us any trouble, I'll spread the word that you're jealous over Brian rejecting your advances. I'll make sure every mother that has the money to pay for a nanny knows your name and the fact that you tried to get involved with my husband. What do you think that will do for your career?"

"Threatening me only makes you look more guilty, Penelope." Blu tried to stand her ground as the woman crossed her arms.

"Sam turned me down. He was a good man, who just wasn't interested in me. Brian had no reason to be jealous, nor would he ever be. Trust me. He was much more interested in what other women were doing, than what I was doing. Now if you'll excuse me, I'm going to collect my kids and let Maddie know that she is off for the night."

"What? Why?"

"Do you think I'm blind, Blu? Maddie pleaded with me to come here tonight; I wouldn't be here otherwise. I know you two are friends, and I know that the two of you set me up so that you could accuse me of this ridiculous crime that you've concocted in your mind. I won't tolerate that kind of deceit. I need some time to think about whether Maddie still has a job."

CHAPTER 25

Penelope stalked off toward the go-karts.

Blu's stomach churned. She scrambled for her phone to try to text Maddie a warning before she was blindsided by Penelope. Before she had a chance to text, the phone slid right out of her hands and fell to the ground. She bent down to grab it and when she stood up again, Maddie was right in front of her with Marley and Joey in tow.

"I can't believe you did that, Blu!"

"I'm sorry, Maddie." Blu sent the children onto a nearby train ride and then turned to face her friend. "I didn't expect this to happen. I really am sorry."

"How could you flat out accuse her of murder? You asked me to set up an opportunity to talk to her, not accuse her. You might not realize this, but if I lose this job, I'm really out of luck. Why would you put me at risk like that?"

"I'm sorry, I really thought I would get her to confess." Blu blinked back tears. "I never meant to get you into trouble, Maddie, you know that. I only wanted this job to be good for you. I don't know how things have gotten so out of control. I was so sure that I was right about Penelope and Brian, but I guess I was wrong. I got caught up in the idea that they are rich and powerful, and I was blinded to the real culprit. But I think I've finally figured out the truth."

"I don't want to hear about it, Blu. As far as I'm concerned, you need to stay out of this. You've put a lot of people at risk, all because of this theory that you have, and that isn't right. These are people's lives, not some way to make up for your lost education."

"That's rather cruel, Maddie, and unfair. That's not what I'm doing here. I'm trying to solve the murder of a good man."

"A good man that died. You've found no real proof of murder. When are you going to give this up? What if Penelope talks to Rachel? What do you think will happen to your job? Blu, you know I love you. You're my friend and you always will be, but I'm very upset with you right now. I think you've taken this a little too far, and to be honest, I'm worried about the way you're behaving. It's not like you to have a drink with Brian—to make it seem like you'd offer him more than that. Yeah, Penelope told me that too."

"You're chastising *me* for flirting?" Blu's eyes widened.

"You're not me. Yes, I was being risky, but you

snapped me out of it. Now I'm trying to do the same for you. Are you going to listen, or are you going to go down in flames?"

"Isn't that a bit dramatic?" Blu turned away from her. "I'm not going to let a man's death go unnoticed because it's safer to keep my mouth shut."

"You're too blinded by what you think is true to see the actual truth. You're ruining your life and the lives of others with your meddling. If you're bored, write a novel, don't invent a fictional crime!"

"I thought you, of all people, would believe me." Blu blinked back tears as the weight of her friend's words struck her.

"You know what I believe, Blu?" Maddie met her eyes. "I believe that you think you're doing what's right, but you're not. You didn't choose to become a journalist. You chose to become a nanny. So why aren't those kids and their family your first priority? Why are you putting all of them at risk by investigating something that will only lead to more heartbreak?"

"Maddie, please. What if I'm right, though? What if Sam was murdered and no one ever knows the truth?"

Maddie frowned and shook her head. "Don't you think if he was, someone would have seen something— someone would know something?"

The question reminded Blu about the windbreaker. She took a deep breath before she spoke again. "Maddie, I know I don't deserve it, and you're so very angry at me right now, but can you do me one last favor? Then I promise, I won't involve you in this at all any more."

"What?" Maddie frowned.

"Could you look in Brian's closet for a windbreaker?"

"What does that have to do with anything?"

"Just please check for me." Blu pleaded. "Then that will be all. I'll never breathe a word about this to you again."

"Fine." Maddie sighed. "I'll check. But Brian has a lot of clothes, Blu."

"Thank you. I promise, if you lose your job over this, I'll do whatever it takes to get you another one."

Maddie frowned and opened her arms to Blu. "I know you didn't mean for any of this to happen."

Blu waited for Maddie to say that she forgave her, but Maddie didn't speak another word. She just pulled away and walked off.

"Blu, can we ride the train again?" Joey jumped up and down at her side. "Marley threw up!"

"What?" Blu looked down at Marley, whose shirt was speckled with grime. "Oh, baby, I'm so sorry." She hadn't thought about Marley's motion sickness before she put her on the train ride. Just as Maddie said, she wasn't paying attention to the family that needed her.

"Let's go get you a nice new shirt, hm?"

"Okay." Marley smiled. "Can I have ice cream too?"

"How about after we're done with the rides?"

Marley giggled.

Blu spent the rest of the night focused on the two kids that she'd sworn to help raise and protect.

The next morning Blu's stomach was still in knots over her conversation with Maddie the night before. She tried to ignore her feelings and stay focused on the crime. She wanted to make sure that she was right this time.

The kids had a birthday party to attend, so she made sure that they were dressed appropriately and fed a good breakfast.

After dropping them off, she knew she had some time to figure out her next step. If Penelope was telling the truth and Brian had no reason to be jealous of her relationship with Sam, then she needed to face the facts. As awful as it made her feel inside, she suspected that there was only one other person that could have been on the beach the morning that Sam died.

CHAPTER 26

Before going to Kayla's, Blu stopped off at the beach house. The kids still had a few more hours at their birthday party. She didn't think anyone else would be home for some time. With the house to herself she felt comfortable doing some research in the middle of the living room.

She opened up her computer and began to search into Kayla's history. It was clear that Kayla was not shy about social media. In fact there were so many selfies that Blu had to filter them out. She searched for one post in particular. When she came across it she smiled with victory.

The post described Kayla's heartbreak over Sam leaving her. She blasted the wealthy side of town and talked about the temptation of money being stronger than the force of true love. It was all quite dramatic and very angry. It was clear that Kayla was not happy with the choice that Sam had made.

Blu tracked Kayla's social media posts over the past days and they became all about grief, the loss of her true love, and how she would never love again.

On a hunch Blu dug into the newspaper articles for the local community for the past few summers. She was not surprised when she came across an article about an eighteen-year-old Kayla being arrested for disorderly conduct. Reading between the lines of the article, it was easy to surmise that it was a dispute between Kayla and another woman over Sam's attention. She had a history of violent behavior and jealousy. Kayla was also still young enough not to think through the consequences of her actions—to instead act on impulse.

"Kayla, it's time to tell the truth."

She checked for Kayla's most recent address. Then she closed her computer and headed out.

Blu kept a constant watch on the time. She made sure that her cell phone was on. She didn't want to risk getting caught up in the investigation and missing the pick-up time for the kids' birthday party.

When she reached Kayla's neighborhood, she parked down the road from her house. With casual steps she walked toward Kayla's house. A part of her expected Kayla not to be there. She expected that this loose end would be just that—a loose—perpetually unraveled—end.

Instead, when she reached the end of the driveway, she noticed a very different scene. Kayla was right there, surrounded by boxes.

Blu stood back as Kayla loaded a box into the back of her truck.

"Are you moving, Kayla?"

"I am." She glanced over at her. "Do I know you?"

"No. I'm just a nanny for a family that stays in one of the beach houses."

"Oh, you're one of those." She picked up another box. "Come to see the sideshow?"

"What do you mean?"

Kayla dropped the box down into the bed of the truck with a loud thump. She brushed off her hands and turned to face Blu. "Here I am. The woman who had everything. I had a man who loved me—not some guy who thought I looked good or wanted to marry me for my cooking. But a man who loved me—all of me— because of who I am. I had what most women never get to experience. And, like a fool, I sat back and let them take him from me."

"What makes you think that someone took him from you?"

Kayla moved forward so that she could look directly into Blu's eyes. "Sam would never leave me, not if he had any other choice."

"But didn't he break up with you?"

"He broke up with me, because he didn't want to hurt me. That's how much he loved me. I told him he was an idiot, that he didn't need to end things, but he said that he couldn't even consider cheating on me. That devil woman tempted him with more money than anyone could turn down. His poor parents were a month away from being evicted from their new place. What was he going to do?"

"I bet that burned you up on the inside, Kayla. I bet you had the one thing in the world that you thought none of those rich spoiled women would ever have. You had the love of a good and loyal man. Until one of those women found a way to take him from you. When that happened, I bet you couldn't stand it. The hurt was too much, the anger overtook you, and you made a plan."

"A plan?" She stared at Blu. "Yes, I made a plan to win Sam back, to prove to him that I would never care about what he'd done."

"Or maybe you made a plan to make sure that no one else could have him. If you couldn't have him, then you wanted to make sure that no one else ever would."

"What?" Kayla's eyes flew wide open. "Do you think I murdered Sam?"

"Well, not with your bare hands." Blu crossed her arms. "You're much too small to be able to do that, and besides that, I don't believe that you would have been able to go through with it. No, I think you paid someone else to do it. I think you decided that Sam was better off dead than as Penelope's puppet."

Kayla slapped Blu right across the face. The impact was so unexpected that Blu cried out and stumbled back. In her entire life she'd never been struck by another person. She pressed her palm against her cheek, which burned with pain.

"Kayla! What are you doing?" AJ charged out of Kayla's house and grabbed the young woman around the waist. Kayla fought so hard to get free and attack Blu again that AJ had to lift her right up off the ground.

Blu noticed the ripple of AJ's muscles. She also didn't overlook the fact that he had been in Kayla's house.

"That's right, so you paid AJ to do it, right?"

"To do what?" AJ looked at Blu and then glared at Kayla. "Don't you dare bite me! What is going on here?"

"She thinks I murdered Sam! She thinks I paid someone to kill him!"

AJ abruptly released Kayla. She almost fell to the ground when he did. He grabbed her arm to steady her.

"What?" He stared at Blu. "Is that true? You think I murdered Sam? Blu, what are you talking about?"

CHAPTER 27

Blu chewed on the edge of her tongue. When AJ looked at her like that, she had a hard time thinking anything. She couldn't figure out why he had such an impact on her, but he did.

"Well, you had as much to lose as Kayla did—in fact more. You had as much to lose as Penelope and Brian did. Didn't you? If Sam ran his mouth off about what happened upstairs, what would happen then, AJ? Would you lose the bar? Would you go to jail? You probably wouldn't have the chance, because the elite would have you taken out of the picture before you even had a chance to hire a lawyer. So when Kayla came to you with a plan, it was pretty much a win-win, wasn't it? Kayla gets her revenge, Sam takes his secret to a watery grave, and it all looks like an accident."

"Seriously. I should let her have a go at you." He continued to hold tight to Kayla's arm. "Not many people still manage to surprise me, Blu, but you've done just that.

"Because I figured it all out?" She braced herself for Kayla's release.

"Because you couldn't be more wrong about who I am, and I couldn't have been more wrong about who you are." He shook his head with disgust. "To think I tried to help you! You're nuts if you think I had anything to do with killing Sam, and you're downright insane if you think Kayla did."

"I saw the two of you. I saw her paying you money. I'm not insane. I know what I saw."

"Sure you saw it. You saw Kayla paying me for the truck that she was buying from me. That's why I'm here, to get the final paperwork and help her pack her things. She wants to get as far from this place as she can, and I see why now. It's not bad enough that she lost the love of her life, but now she's being accused of being involved in his death? What's wrong with you, Blu?"

Blu took a slight step back. Her cheeks flushed with heat. Could she be wrong? She was so sure that she was right.

"I just thought—"

"—Stop. Please." AJ interrupted her. "Stop thinking about it at all. You've gotten everyone all upset, and you've done nothing to help Sam. Just go back to your beach house and stay out of our business."

"I don't understand." Blu shook her head. "Someone killed Sam."

"Maybe." AJ met her eyes. "But like I said before, we'll never know for sure. I believed for a little while that you might actually be able to figure something out, but now I see that you were just looking to blame the locals. I get it—you don't know me, you want to accuse me of murder. I can tolerate that. But Kayla? She's the only innocent one in all of this. How could you accuse her?"

"She was so angry." Blu frowned.

AJ released Kayla.

Instead of charging toward Blu, Kayla only hung her head. "Wouldn't you be? Haven't you ever been in love, Blu?"

Blu frowned. "No. I haven't."

"Then you can't understand." Kayla's voice was quite as she continued. "They took him from me. Whether they took him by getting him so worked up that he made a mistake, or by finding a cunning way to cover up his murder, isn't going to change the fact that they simply took him. Nothing fixes that."

"But some things can make it worse. Wasn't he already gone before he died, Kayla?"

"No, he wasn't." Kayla blinked back tears. "He would have come back to me. We would have had our lives together. Nothing in this world would make me ever harm a single strand of hair on his head. You don't have to believe me, but it's the truth."

"Either you accept it, or you get off this property." AJ crossed his arms. "The last thing Kayla needs is to be harassed. I suppose you think that I had something to do with all of this, and to be honest with you, I don't care what you think. I don't have anything to prove to you,

Blu, and neither does Kayla."

"No, she's just going on the run, isn't she?" Blu narrowed her eyes. "Isn't that what guilty people do? They get as far from the crime as possible?"

"Enough!" AJ moved in front of Kayla. "Off of this property this instant or I'll have Chief Pitman here in two seconds to arrest you."

"Oh, that's right, I forgot. The police force only does its job when it suits them. I guess that your uncle has a problem with investigating a murder, but he'll be more than happy to show some favor to his favorite nephew."

"Blu, you've lost it." His voice grew quiet. "You've really lost it. Get out of here, or I'll make sure that you're thrown in a holding cell until you come to your senses."

A glimmer of fear flashed through Blu's mind. If she was in a holding cell, who would pick up the kids from the birthday party?

"Fine." She raised her hands into the air. "I'm going."

Blu walked back to her car. She grew more angry with every step. Either a grieving woman was guilty of murder as Blu had just accused, or AJ was heavily involved in the cover-up of Sam's murder. She hated to think that either was true.

She still had a little time before the birthday party was over. Instead of driving back to the house, she headed for the dock.

She needed a chance to clear her mind.

CHAPTER 28

After parking near the dock, Blu checked in with the parents who were hosting the birthday party. The kids had been invited to stay a bit longer to play, so she could relax for a few minutes.

She walked the wooden planks of the dock and looked out over the water. She sat at the end of the dock. She watched the last of the light disappear on the horizon.

In a short amount of time she'd managed to alienate just about everyone, including her best friend Maddie. She wasn't sure if she'd made the right choice by looking into Sam's death. It felt like the right choice, but maybe she was just dead wrong.

The ripple of the water against the dock calmed her, but it didn't change the fact that she was alone. There was a sense of isolation from everyone and everything. At the beginning of the summer, her biggest concern had been sunscreen and skinned knees; now her mind was consumed with what had happened to Sam.

As Kayla had said, were Sam's last thoughts an anguished desire to get to her? It made Blu's heart ache to think so. Who would end a love like that? Who would have the power and the coldness to do that?

"What are you doing out here all alone?"

Blu heard AJ's voice coming from a few feet behind her. She turned to look up at him. The sunlight was so bright that it nearly blinded her. Was that what Sam saw last? The face of someone he knew and trusted?

"Just thinking."

He smiled. "I see that. Would you like to have a drink with me and talk about what's on your mind?"

Blu till didn't know what to make of AJ. Was he someone that could be trusted? Was he a suspect beneath that friendly demeanor?

"After what I did to Kayla? After all those things you said to me?"

"Look, I got a little heated. I'm sorry. I can be overprotective, I've been told. I know that you're only trying to figure out what happened to Sam. I'd like to know what you've figured out so far."

"Alright." She stood up. The only way she could figure out if she could trust AJ was by getting to know him better.

They left the dock and stepped inside the Beach Bum. Just as they settled at a table, Blu's phone rang. When she saw it was Maddie she picked it up right away.

"Maddie? What is it?"

"I just saw a windbreaker hanging in Brian's closet."

"You did?" Blu's eyes widened. "Can you get it?"

"I don't know, but I can tell you that even if I could, it's not going to be worth much to you."

"Why not?"

"He's had it dry cleaned. It's still in the plastic."

"Oh." All of Blu's excitement faded. "But it's there?"

"Yes."

"Can you send me a picture of it?"

"Yes, I can do that. I'll text it to you."

"Thanks, Maddie. I really appreciate you doing this."

"Blu, you know that I adore you. I just don't want to lose my job."

As soon as the picture came through, Blu jumped up from the table.

"What is it, what's wrong?" AJ stood up with her.

"I need to go see someone."

"Why?"

"Never mind. We'll have to postpone that drink."

"Wait, I'm going with you." AJ moved between her and the door of the bar. "I'm not sure what you're up to, but I can't just let you run around town making accusations."

"Fine, if you want to come with me, do. But I'm driving." She rushed past him and out the door.

He followed right on her heels. Blu sped toward Jeffery's house. She never sped or drove recklessly with the kids in the car, so this was a big change for her—not to mention the fact that the police chief's nephew sat beside her, with a clear view of her speedometer.

She parked in Jeffery's driveway, careful to watch for Duke. Jeffery stepped outside and waved to her.

"Blu, what's up?"

"Jeffery, I need to show you a picture."

"I told you I wasn't close enough to see his face." Jeffery looked warily at AJ as he stepped out of the car as well.

"This isn't a picture of a person. Is this the windbreaker that you saw the man wearing?" She held up her phone with the picture of the windbreaker displayed.

"Yes, that's it." Jeffery nodded. "That looks like the jacket the man was wearing on the beach."

"Are you sure?" AJ narrowed his eyes.

"I'm sure. I couldn't see his face, but those bright colors I could see."

"See?" Blu smiled at AJ. "That should be enough proof for your uncle, right?"

"I don't know." AJ shook his head. "This is a beach town. Almost everyone has a windbreaker. I have one." He met her eyes. "Does that make me a murderer?"

"No, of course not." She dropped her gaze. "Could you just talk to your uncle?"

"Alright, I'll see what I can do. Just promise me that you'll wait here until I get a hold of him. Okay?"

"Sure." Blu nodded.

She watched as AJ walked away to make the call. But

who was he calling? Was he calling Kayla to warn her that the murder was about to be solved? Was he really calling his uncle to have her arrested? Or was he warning someone else entirely?

Blu still didn't know why AJ felt so familiar to her. Despite her suspicions, her first instinct was to trust him. But she couldn't take the chance that he was going to get rid of the only evidence that she might have. What if it was Brian on the other end of the line? After all, AJ did run the bar where Brian and Penelope explored the limits of their open marriage.

No, she couldn't wait.

She watched Jeffery toss a ball for Duke. Duke chased it down with his tongue wagging as he ran. The dog knew how to chase down what he wanted.

So did Blu.

As soon as AJ was a safe distance away, she hopped into her car and took off. There was no way she was going to allow time for that windbreaker to disappear.

CHAPTER 29

She pulled up in front of the Rosses' beach house. It was twice the size of the one that she stayed in. It was spotless, with top of the line architecture and perfectly manicured bushes. From the outside it might as well have been a palace, but she knew now that it hid something much darker inside its walls.

She dialed Maddie's number. Maddie answered quickly.

"Hello?"

"Are you home?"

"Yes, the kids are in the pool. Why?"

"I'm out front."

"What? Why?"

"Can you bring me the windbreaker?"

"Oh, Blu, I don't know. This is crazy."

Blu stepped out of the car and tightened her grip on the phone. "Please, Maddie. This might be my last chance to make this stick. If this doesn't work, I'm going to have to give up."

Maddie sighed. "Alright, I'll let you in. Just give me a

minute to get the kids out of the pool."

While Blu waited on the doorstep, she heard a siren wail up the street. She turned to see a patrol car skid to a stop in front of the house. From the opposite direction a dark blue sedan pulled up.

Her heart fluttered as she realized that the driver of the patrol car was Chief Pitman. AJ was in the passenger seat. He glared at her through the windshield. She glanced away from his angry stare. But what made things worse was the driver of the blue sedan. It was Brian Ross.

Brian jumped out of his car and began walking toward her in the same moment that Chief Pitman and AJ climbed out of the patrol car. Blu was surrounded.

"What's wrong? Is it one of the kids?" Brian sounded out of breath. His face grew a darker red with every second that passed.

"No, nothing like that, Mr. Ross." Chief Pitman pulled off his hat and held it in his hand. "Could I speak with you for a moment?" His nature with Brian was far more charming than it had ever been with Blu.

Brian settled his gaze on Blu and then looked back at Chief Pitman. "Is this because of her? Something she said? Did she tell you that she came on to me and I turned her down?" He waved a hand in her direction. "She's nuts!"

Blu opened her mouth to protest, but AJ shot her a look that silenced her. His teeth clenched so tight that she could see the movement of his jaw. Blu pursed her lips and tilted her head toward the door.

Just as she was about to point out where the windbreaker was, Maddie appeared at the door.

"Maddie? Do you know anything about this?" Brian's fury was clear in the tone of his voice.

Maddie visibly winced and Blu mouthed an apology to her.

"Mr. Ross, do you happen to own a windbreaker?" Chief Pitman put his hat back on top of his head and lowered his voice.

"What?" Brian looked at him. "What if I do? Why does it matter?"

"It probably doesn't. Can you please just answer the question, Mr. Ross?"

"Yes, fine. I just bought one recently. I haven't even worn it yet."

"Could we see it? Just for a second, Mr. Ross? Then we can put this craziness to rest." Chief Pitman smiled. "That's all it will take."

Brian stared at him for a long moment. His brow furrowed.

Blu braced herself as she expected Brian to put up a fight.

Instead he just nodded. "Alright, if that's what it will take to make this craziness end. But when I prove to you that there's nothing interesting about my windbreaker, I want her arrested for harassment." He jabbed his finger in Blu's direction.

Blu took a sharp breath.

"Absolutely," said the chief. "I would be glad to ensure that this young woman's poor behavior is dealt with."

"Good." Brian smirked. "Why don't you come with me? We can all look at it together."

"Perfect." Chief Pitman nodded.

"You too, Blu." Brian smiled at her. "I wouldn't want there to be a single doubt in your mind about me. That way when you're sitting in your jail cell, you'll have plenty of time to think about how wrong you were."

Blu's heart dropped. She studied Chief Pitman for any sign of reassurance that he wasn't serious. Chief Pitman refused to even look in her direction.

Maddie led the way and AJ lingered behind the others. Blu stepped up beside him.

"I told you to wait." He locked eyes with her.

Blu didn't say a word. She moved past him and followed the others into the house.

Brian marched right into his bedroom and opened his closet. "There it is." He chuckled. "Is it illegal to have bad taste?"

"No." Chief Pitman ran his finger and thumb along the scruff of his beard. "But I thought you said you just bought the windbreaker?"

"I did. I always have my new items dry-cleaned before I wear them. I mean, the thought of putting on something that hasn't been properly cleaned—well, it makes me very uncomfortable."

"Ah." Chief Pitman nodded. "I see. I suppose if there was any evidence on the windbreaker it's gone now."

"Why would there be any evidence on it?" Brian glared at him. "I didn't do anything to anyone."

"I understand." Chief Pitman gestured to the door. 'We'll leave you to your peace."

"Wait!" Blu stepped forward.

"Blu, enough." AJ's eyes snapped toward her. "There's nothing that can be done."

"I've been a nanny long enough to know one thing." She walked over to the closet and plucked the windbreaker from the rod.

"Don't!" Brian warned.

"What is it?" Chief Pitman looked at her with interest.

"Brian, you claimed that you never wore this? Not even once?"

"Not even once." Brian shook his head. "This is getting to be pathetic."

"Well, as someone who has spent many summers on the beach I can tell you that no amount of washing—no amount of dry cleaning—ever gets all the sand out of pockets." She lifted the plastic that covered the windbreaker. "So why don't we just have a look?"

"I don't want her pawing all over my things!"

"I'll do it." Chief Pitman took the windbreaker from Blu. "You don't mind, do you, Brian? If you're telling the truth, there shouldn't be a trace of sand in these pockets."

"Fine." Brian shoved his hands deep into his pockets. "Look all you want."

Chief Pitman slid his hand into one of the pockets. He paused, and then looked over at Brian. "Do you want to change your story?"

"No, sir." Brian locked eyes with him.

"Are you sure?" Chief Pitman pulled his hand out of the pocket and rubbed sand from his fingertips.

"That doesn't prove anything!" Brian growled.

"It proves that you were on the beach that morning. It proves that you lied about being there." Blu shook her head. "What I don't understand is why? It doesn't seem like you were jealous of Sam's relationship with Penelope."

"Oh please." Brian pressed his palms to his forehead. "Look, how much is it going to take to handle this? I'll get my checkbook out right now."

CHAPTER 30

Chief Pitman shifted his hips and rested his hand on his gun holster. "I can't really calculate that without knowing the whole story."

Brian rolled his eyes. "It doesn't matter. There isn't a shred of evidence against me."

"Except what our witness who saw you in that windbreaker heard you say to Sam." Blu brushed off AJ's restraining hand and stepped forward.

Brian arched an eyebrow. "Oh? What was that?"

"You were upset, but not because Sam rejected your wife, or because Penelope was in love with him. You were upset because Sam wasn't going to keep his mouth shut. Isn't that right?"

A grimace rippled across Brian's perfect features. "No."

"Isn't it?" Blu smiled. "Of all the things in the world that you value, there's only one thing that you would kill to protect, right? Your reputation."

"It wasn't my fault!" Brian roared, which drew the

attention of everyone around him. "All he had to do was accept the pay-off, just like everyone else always did. He signed the paperwork, didn't he? Didn't he, AJ?"

AJ balled his hands into fists. "That didn't give you the right to kill him, Brian! Why would you do something like that?"

"Because Sam wasn't the only man that Penelope was interested in. She and Ian West were seeing one another."

"So?" Blu frowned.

"So, Ian was married too. Sam knew that. When Penelope wouldn't take no for an answer, Sam threatened to tell Ian's wife about Penelope. If he did, it would get out to everyone. There would be no stopping it. It would make Penelope look weak, and it would ruin her business."

"And that's a reason to kill a man?" Blu narrowed her eyes. "He was trying to be honest."

"All he had to do was take the money. When he turned down Penelope's offer, and then mine, I knew that things were out of control. I knew that there was only one option to make it right. I did it to protect her."

"Don't lie, Brian, not now. Don't lie when you know that you did it to protect yourself, and your lifestyle. You like the freedom that Penelope gives you, you like the money, and all of that was going to disappear if Sam spoke the truth."

"I was just going to scare him." Brian looked down at

his own hands. They trembled as he stared at them. "I was just going to hold him under the water long enough to get my point across. But he was stronger than I expected. I had to use the surfboard to hold him down—and the cord got tangled. When I tried to bring him to the surface, he fought me. He almost pulled me under." He looked up at Chief Pitman. "I tried to pull him up. Don't you see? It really was just an accident."

"No." Blu glared at him. "An accident that would never have happened if someone didn't create a dangerous situation. It wasn't an accident. It was murder."

"We're going to need to clear the room." Chief Pitman spoke into his radio to summon backup. Then he turned Brian to face the wall.

"I should go check on the kids," Maddie mumbled.

"I'll go with you." Blu linked her arm through Maddie's and guided her out of the room.

"I can't believe it's true. I can't believe it." Maddie shook her head. "How can this be happening, Blu?"

"There will never be a good explanation for it, Maddie. The important thing now is that we protect the children as much as possible from what their father has done."

"You knew, didn't you, Blu? Somehow you knew the entire time."

"I didn't know as much as you think. I wasn't sure until the very end. I thought I was about to experience life behind bars."

"Blu?" AJ stepped out in the hallway with them.

"Yes?"

"Can I steal you away for just a moment?"

"It's okay." Maddie nodded. "'I've got to call Penelope."

Once Maddie was headed down the stairs, Blu turned back to face AJ. "I know, I know—you told me to wait."

AJ studied her for a long moment. "You know, you were right about me."

"What?" Blu's eyes widened. Was he still somehow involved in the murder?

"I've been turning a blind eye to what happens at the bar, because the money is good. I'm going to change that. From now on, the only thing exchanged in the elite section will be alcohol and beer nuts. Maybe if I had been more honest from the start, this wouldn't have happened to Sam."

"It's not your fault, AJ. It's no one's fault but Brian's. He's the one who made the choice to take the life of another person—an innocent man."

"Maybe." AJ grimaced. "But I can't help but wonder if things might have been different."

"A million things could be changed to save Sam's life, but now it's too late for that. He'll have his justice, and a dangerous man will be in prison. You played a big part in making that happen," Blu said.

"I guess." He slipped his hands into his pockets.

"Don't forget, you still owe me that drink."

"Oh, yes." Blu's heart suddenly dropped. She checked the time on her phone. "Oh no, I have to pick up the kids!"

She ran down the stairs and out the door to her car. With a quick wipe of her eyes, she drove to the birthday party.

Maybe she had solved a murder, but all that really mattered to her was making sure that Marley and Joey made it home to their parents—happy and safe.